W9-DDI-307

HOME
home

LISA ALLEN-AGOSTINI

HOME

home

DELACORTE PRESS

Text copyright © 2020 by Lisa Allen-Agostini
Jacket art copyright © 2020 by Julia Kuo

All rights reserved. Published in the United States by Delacorte Press, an imprint of Random House Children's Books, a division of Penguin Random House LLC, New York. Originally published in paperback in Great Britain by Papillote Press, London, in 2018.

Delacorte Press is a registered trademark and the colophon is a trademark of Penguin Random House LLC.

Visit us on the Web! GetUnderlined.com

Educators and librarians, for a variety of teaching tools, visit us at RHTeachersLibrarians.com

Library of Congress Cataloging-in-Publication Data is available upon request.
ISBN 978-1-9848-9358-1 (hc) — ISBN 978-1-9848-9359-8 (glb) —
ISBN 978-1-9848-9360-4 (ebook)

The text of this book is set in 11.3-point Adobe Garamond Pro.
Interior design by Cathy Bobak

Printed in the United States of America
10 9 8 7 6 5 4 3 2 1
First Edition

Dedicated to the memory of my parents,

Rito and Dolsie

CHAPTER
ONE

That sound; that burbling, bubbling sound. That ringtone was possibly the most annoying sound in the whole world. But it was my lifeline to home.

I hit the big green button. Akilah's face popped up on my screen. She whispered, "Hey, you. What's going on?" Akilah was in church clothes, practically shining in a prim little cardigan over a modest dress. I could just see her collar and buttons. She was rushing out of church as we spoke. Her mom would eat that up. Yet another reason for her mother to hate the reviled best friend: I made Akilah leave while the service was going on.

All these thoughts rushed through me between spasms of terror. Those clutching, needle-sharp pains in my stomach had started, and before I dissolved into a puddle of tears and snat I'd had the good sense to send Akilah a Skype message: *Not doing so great. Be nice to talk.*

What can I say? I have a rare gift for understatement.

Lucky for me, she had her phone on—a no-no, as far as her mom was concerned. "Phones off in church" is a strict rule, as any churchgoer knows. Lucky for me, Akilah realized I was having a hard time and had defied the rule to be there when she knew I needed her. Lucky for me, she was a great friend.

She was my best friend—and she was my only friend.

"God," I groaned. "Ki-ki, I'm dying."

"No, girl, you're not dying," she responded. She was whispering and walking at the same time; and behind her the sunlight was blinding. She stopped and stood in the dappled shade of a mango tree, its dark green leaves rustling noisily in the breeze. "What's the matter?"

"Nothing," I said. "Everything."

"That's not an answer," she scolded me. "What is causing you to feel like this right now?" She was familiar with my panic attacks: I'd get sweaty, my heart would race, I'd feel breathless and terrified and end up sobbing for hours. It wasn't a good look. What amazed me was that she was always ready to give me a shoulder to cry on. Before I'd gotten to Canada, hers was the only one I had.

"I am walking to the bus stop, trying to get home . . . ," I started to explain before trailing off.

"And?" She waited for me to answer. It took a while.

I took another step on the long white highway.

It was about seventeen degrees Celsius, warm for Canadians but cold for me; I haven't gotten used to the weather yet; though we use the same temperature scale as Canada, they use the lower parts much more than we did. For them seventeen degrees is a nice day, and they put on shorts and tank tops and walk around like I would at the beach or in the park, but for me, it's just another wrap-up-tight day, wear-my-coat day, feel-too-cold day. Home was never this cold, even on the chilliest nights, even up in the high hills of Trinidad's Northern Range where mist covers the road in the early morning.

Almost as though in sympathy with the windy day in Trinidad, the wind picked up. I felt it blowing through my short black hair, trying to ruffle it and failing. Canadian wind, oh you don't know anything about hair like mine. You haven't seen enough of it in this quiet backwoods on the prairie. You think my hair is gonna just submit to you, flip and dance in you, fly and move in you? Not my hair. It's worked too hard for too long to just give in to you. It's tough hair, wiry hair, strong hair, hair that won't be cowed by some damn prairie wind. No sirree, not this hair.

"Sweetie?" Akilah asked sharply.

When I'm having a panic attack I can find it hard to carry on a conversation. My thoughts become confused and all the words become tangled in my mind, a ball of stifled self-expression. So I tried to focus on the road I was walking on.

A long concrete road, it was four lanes wide and full of zooming, beeping, clanking, whooshing cars, buses, and trucks. Trucks especially. They weren't allowed to drive on the cross streets, only roads that ran the length of this part of Edmonton.

The trucks were big, lumbering, trundling things that passed too close to me as I walked. The pavement and road were the same color, the same texture. Home home, roads were black, the way roads should be. Roads back home were made of asphalt mined from Trinidad's Pitch Lake. Not here. Edmonton's bone-white, cold concrete highway scared me in some primal way. This wasn't a road into anything good; it couldn't be. And I'd never seen so many trucks. They were like huge devils with horns blaring and fangs in their grilles, evil grins, bad intentions, bearing down on me from behind, leering at me as they powered past, warning me they'd be back for me—not now but at some unspecified, very real date in the future. The wind they raised was bitter and hot, not like the wind that normally blew cold, odorless, and sterile. The wind blown from the sides of the trucks was dusty and tasted like ashes in my mouth.

Houses ran alongside the road. Stretching over the four lanes every now and then was a big blue road sign that told me where I was. I also kept track by counting the street signs at each corner. Twenty-First Street. Twentieth Street. Nineteenth Street. The streets seemed inordinately far apart. I had four more blocks to walk before I turned in to the bus station.

"What's going on?" Akilah was now insistent. All she'd heard was the jagged sound of my breath as I freaked out, abrupt inhalations and shaky exhalations that would stop me from screaming. I must have looked awful.

"I'm in the middle of nowhere."

"Why are you walking in the middle of nowhere?"

"I should take a bus from the city to the station, then from the station to home," I confessed. "But I never remember quickly enough which bus to take to get to the station. I feel like an idiot standing there staring at the transit map. I keep some schedules in my pocket, but . . ."

It sounds stupid, but I was always, always easily flustered when I had choices to make, even simple, everyday ones. Should I have rice or pasta? Lettuce or cabbage? The Fourteen or the Eighteen? My choice could kill me. At least, that was what it felt like. And please don't get me started on multiple-choice tests. Exams were always hell. I never knew how to decide things.

So instead of trying to figure out which bus to take when my brain was stuck in a goo of confusion, I walked to the little bus station, with its heavy, warm air panting out of buses that crouched in a waiting lane, engines still running. Meanwhile, the drivers used the bathroom or made phone calls to their families, or just chilled with other workers in the small office behind the bulletproof glass of the customer service counter.

The bus schedules in my pocket, clutched too tight too many times, had become grimy and old through the weeks I'd used them. No matter how many times I took the bus, I always forgot which one I needed. I sat and took really deep breaths, I could remember that mornings my bus was the Fourteen, going north into the city; and evenings my bus was the Eighteen, going south into the suburbs. But when I was in the grip of a panic attack there was no way I could remember that, as ridiculous as it might sound. I had to pull out both schedules every time I walked to catch a bus. I had to smooth out the wrinkles, squint down at them and look to see which bus went where. And as soon as I put them back into my pocket I'd forget again. Which bus goes where? What time is it running? Am I in the right place?

Having a panic disorder really sucks.

"You're not an idiot," Akilah consoled me. "In fact, you're one of the smartest people I know. Quick . . . what's the capital of Moldavia?"

"Moldavia isn't a country anymore. You're thinking of Moldova. And the capital is Chişinău."

"Kitchen-what?" The strange pronunciation slayed her, her laughter momentarily almost distracting me from the blood pounding in my ears, the fear narrowing my vision.

"Chişinău. Google it," I growled, ashamed that I could instantly recall dotish trivia like that but couldn't figure out which bus to hop on.

Akilah was on a mission, though. She saw right through my embarrassment and shook her head in exaggerated mock disapproval. "You see? Which fourteen-year-old Trini girl not only knows that Moldova exists, but knows the name of its capital city and how to pronounce it? You're a genius!"

"Meh," I said dismissively. "Such a genius I can't remember how to get home. Every. Single. Day."

She laughed, but it was a sympathetic chuckle, not a jeer. Trinidadians made jokes about everything. We laughed at life. It was one of the things that made Trinis special, I thought. But my sense of humor wasn't helping at that moment.

"Could you just talk to me?" I begged. "Tell me what's going on with school and church and everything. How did you do in end-of-term tests?"

"Oooh . . . I got a B in chemistry," she began in disgust. "Mr. Look Loy said my project was disappointing. Can you imagine? I never got a B in my life. . . ."

As Akilah started talking to distract me, I noticed the breeze even more. This afternoon wind seemed determined to get to me, to find something it could interfere with. It crept under my jeans and my high collar, trying to penetrate the layers of fabric to reach my skin. I could feel it swirling below my clothes. But I was prepared, too wily for the wind. I had on long underwear.

Summer in Edmonton is not hot, but it's not cold. Unless, that is, you're used to living in a furnace. I was. I was from the Caribbean, where an average day might easily be twice as hot as an average Edmonton summer day. What was sixteen degrees when you were really built for thirty-two, when your blood was as warm as the Gulf of Paria when the sun was shining down on the chalky finger of San Fernando Hill? Here, I was always cold, bundling myself up in layers and obscenely more layers, wearing all the clothes in my wardrobe at once.

Like a real Trini, Aunty Jillian laughed at me all the time about that. She and her partner, Aunty Julie, couldn't understand why I was always kitted out like a bag lady in sweater, shirt, long underwear, jeans, and sneakers after my arrival in Edmonton. On really bad days, like today, I wore my coat, a long velveteen number I bought at a thrift store because I wasn't going to be in this city much longer and I was sure nobody wanted to spend real money on my "penance" clothes. Already Jillian and Julie had paid for my trip to Canada, had welcomed me into their home, were taking care of me. I felt I owed them too much to accept an expensive, brand-new fall coat when it wasn't yet fall. I'd have to go back to Trinidad soon anyway.

My thrifted velveteen coat was a rich electric blue, the color of the sky at home when it was just about sunset—not on the side with the lightshow of the sun going down in an orange blaze of glory but the other one, the side where night is creeping up and day is already a memory. The sky could be such an elegant, intense, impenetrable, and unutterably lovely blue. When I saw the coat on the hanger, it seemed it was waiting for me. Everybody laughed at my purchase, especially Jillian, who called it my Princess Di coat. In truth it was too formal, and pretty old-fashioned, but I didn't care. It fit and I loved the color and the smooth, short nap of the velveteen. The lining was genuine silk, which was heavenly against my hands.

Plus, when you're wearing a big, thick coat it feels like it's easy to disappear.

"English and Lit were super easy, like I told you. Oh, and I can't remember exactly what I wrote for the first Literature essay, the one on Julius Caesar—something about portents, I think— but Miss Ramsubir said she wants to publish it in the *School Tie* next—"

"What's the *School Tie*?" I asked. She'd never mentioned it before.

"The school magazine. She wants me to write for it. . . ."

I was a bit closer to the bus station and Akilah's voice had calmed me down a little. I could pay attention to small things again, like the flowers in front of people's houses, or the faint warmth of the sunshine on my face.

"Maths wasn't terrible. I got two questions wrong in the long paper. I hate graphs." Akilah groaned theatrically.

I kept walking, making a fist with my free hand and sticking it into my coat's silk-lined pocket. My short nails pressed pink crescents into my palm, the pain keeping me from screaming out when the scary trucks passed with their horns blaring *boooohhh-hhppp!* Devil trucks.

"Nobody ever stops me or says hello or anything," I suddenly said to Akilah. "I literally walk around here and nobody says a word. Canadians are so into their own space that they try not to interfere with anybody else's."

Akilah, used to my disjointed thoughts during my panic attacks, picked up the ball and ran with it. "Not like the *macos* we have here in Trinidad," she teased. "Always minding your business. Aunty Cynthia would have got about three phone calls by now from the neighborhood *macos* if you were home and going down the highway."

It was true, sort of. At home—home home, not here—people stopped and talked to perfect strangers. Yes, the *macos* minded your business like it was their human right to do so. But at least you smiled at them and saw in their faces some emotion. Here, a strange and hostile silence fell when the occasional person came near me. Not that I saw too many people on this terrifying jaunt.

"Nobody even walks here either," I told her, and moaned. "I'm a freak. Aunty Jillian and her girlfriend would have picked me up from the city if I had asked them to, but that would have meant them driving out of their way." I bit my lip. "I don't want to be too much trouble."

"Oh, sweetie," Akilah sighed. The light behind her dimmed as the sun ducked behind a cloud. "You know they wouldn't mind."

"Well, they don't work in the city!" I argued. "They would have to leave the house, get me, and turn around. I don't want to be a nuisance."

I was being dishonest. Yes, they did work from home. They

had a computer-based business that they ran from the cool, dry basement of their little house in the suburbs, my temporary home for the past several weeks. But I knew they would have been happy to pick me up from the city. I told myself maybe things would change once I got more used to being in Edmonton, that maybe I wouldn't feel like such a burden, crashing in and ruining their perfect lives while I served out my penance here. Maybe.

It was nearly summer. School was out. Trying to make myself invisible in the new city where I lived, but knowing I couldn't just stay in bed as much as I wished I could, I spent my days at the library, reading. I liked books, probably because I spent so much time alone with them when I was a child. Books don't judge you. Books don't think you're awkward or wrong, and they don't give you that cut eye you get from your mother when you should be washing dishes but you're reading instead. Libraries made me feel at home. When I wasn't reading, sometimes I went to the gym. Sometimes I went swimming at the community pool. Sometimes I went to a museum; there were a bunch of them in Edmonton, unlike Trinidad, which had only a few in the whole country. This place was so strange, so new. Sometimes, when I could stand to do it, I just walked around and listened to the city breathe.

This routine worked well with the reason I was here in the first place. I was officially in Edmonton on holiday, recovering from my recent troubles. In reality, my mom had shunted me off here. I was half a world away from home to hide until the end of the school term, which I had started off in a hospital bed.

It was now June and I was tired of my penance.

Why did I call it penance? Because my mother was so ashamed

of my illness, when she sent me away to recover it felt like she was punishing me. So: penance.

Penance was hard. I missed the sunshine, I missed my room, I missed my house, I missed walking on High Street, San Fernando. I missed Akilah. I did not miss school. And I didn't miss my mother as much as I should. Every time I thought of her I remembered the sour and hurt expression on her face when I was in hospital. She didn't believe that my illness was real. She felt it was a personal indictment of her and my upbringing. It was clinical depression. I tried to tell her, the doctor tried to tell her, Aunt Jillian tried to tell her. Depression is an illness. It had nothing to do with her. It was inside me, like some kind of code in my basic programming. My operating software told my body and my mind that I was unhappy. It didn't matter if she was a good mother or not.

I was still walking, alone because of my penance. Akilah was still on Skype, too, her quiet, sure voice talking to me, telling me, "Don't worry, chick. You will get there, you will not get lost, you will find the bus station, you will catch a bus, you will get home." She broke off, mumbling, "And Mummy will kill me if I don't go back inside."

Sure enough, I heard sharp high heels clicking on the other side of the call. "Akilah! Get off that phone! What have I said about leaving church to talk to your friends?" Aunty Patsy's stern voice brooked no discussion.

"Got to go!" Akilah whispered, swiftly sending me a kiss and a wink before ending the call.

I clutched my phone in a sweaty hand. Akilah was gone, but

her voice had helped; I could breathe again. The road wasn't so terrifying anymore.

The summer flowers outside each house on this road were brighter than I would have imagined when I was living in the Caribbean. I had always thought of Canada—or any temperate place, actually—as dull and somehow less colorful than home. I had been surprised to see that the blossoms could be as red, as yellow, and as blue as the flowers in my own yard in Trinidad. Not caring to learn the names of the flora I wouldn't be around much longer, I called these Canadian blooms by their sizes, shapes, and colors: the big pink one, the small blue one, the orange one with the dizzy, swirling petals. The wind had more success with them than with my wiry, tight curls. Those flowers danced in it, their little heads nodding and twisting in the strong breeze.

All the houses I passed were similar, though. Once, before I got the courage to take the bus at all, I tried walking straight home from the city. Twenty-four blocks didn't seem like much—and it only took about fifteen minutes by car to get from the heart of town to my aunt's house, so I figured I would be fine. Uh-uh. It was long. In fact, in my mind I called it the Day of the Longest Walk. I walked for three hours and just kept counting corners and counting corners until in frustration I stopped a little kid and asked where Second Street was.

Turned out I was standing on it, right by Aunty Jillian's house. The houses all looked exactly the same to me, and I simply hadn't recognized hers. But there it was: a small, brownish-white cottage surrounded by a perfect, jewel-green lawn and tubs of summer blooms, separated from its neighbors by hedges and chain-link fencing. On one side of the house was a black-doored garage with a car inside; another car was parked outside in the driveway. Aunt Jillian had a couple of garden gnomes cavorting in a Japanese-looking grotto she had made of rocks and stones, some dark-green perennial shrub, and pieces of driftwood she had collected on the grayish sand of Vessigny Beach, where she used to go with my mom and their parents when they were small. It was not a shrine, but she tended this grotto carefully, raking it and keeping it looking really nice, washing down the garden gnomes until they shone, even though she constantly made fun of them. I imagined they had secret lives like the singing gnomes in a movie I liked when I was a kid.

On the Day of the Longest Walk, I had been confused, too, because of perspective. I'd never seen Jillian and Julie's house from that angle. I had always driven up into the garage in the passenger seat of their car, and entered the house through the side door in the garage. Nobody used the front door at all, I noticed. Seemed it was only there for decoration. People entered from the deck via the kitchen. From the garage, a side door led to the hallway between the formal living room and the rest of the house. The front door was seldom touched, except by Julie during her Saturday-morning cleaning rampages, when every bit of brass and glass in the house was polished till it gleamed like new. The front door was formal and austere, like the living room into which it opened, and perhaps nobody wanted that feeling of formality to be sullied with ordinary dirt and finger smudges.

Formalities or not, I wished I were there already, and yet I was still walking. I turned a corner, counting streets laterally this time.

I knew the street names by heart now, and ran through them in my head as if I were afraid someday I'd be walking by and someone would have secretly changed them in the night just to confuse me. In my mind I called their names as I passed them: Evergreen, Fir, Pine, Aspen—names of trees I didn't know from home at all, trees I wouldn't recognize by sight. Then the bus station came into view.

Two cops idly watched me approach. They were wearing summer uniforms of short sleeves and short pants, and looked with obvious amusement at my over-padded appearance. I smiled uncomfortably at them and clenched my fists tighter in the pockets of my coat. It was a strange contradiction: I hated how nobody talked to me, but at the same time I didn't really want anybody to talk to me, either. Maybe I was afraid of what I'd say in return. Or maybe I was afraid I'd just turn into a puddle of shame and terror right at their feet. Who knew?

Plus, they were cops. Canada is neighbors with America, and I briefly thought of the black people who'd been shot by law enforcement for doing absolutely nothing but what I was doing— walking. Even that wasn't the same as in Trinidad, where police in jeeps pulled up on young black kids in the street to hassle them, rough them up, scare them, as a matter of course. But they didn't shoot them. I was wary, to say the least.

The taller of the two, a very young blond guy with thick legs, grinned back at my nervous smile. As soon as I was within earshot he asked, "Are you sure you're warm enough?" His question caught me off guard.

"Yes, thanks," I said, bowing my head and trying to avoid him, in case this seeming friendliness was some kind of trick.

It didn't work. Hearing my Caribbean accent, he immediately did what many white Canadians I'd met had done: he asked, "Where are you from?"

"Trinidad," I told him, before scuttling into the sheltered booth of the commuter queue, yearning to get my chilled bones out of the wind and escape from this disturbingly interested policeman.

I quickly warmed up, keeping my eye on the cops on the corner. My heart was still racing, but my palms weren't as sweaty, and my breathing was calming down. I looked at my little watch, which my mother had given me three years ago when I sat for my secondary school entrance exam. A useful present, as you couldn't take the exam with a cell phone as your timer. My mother didn't give me many gifts just because. They were always practical, sensible: a new church dress, new sneakers for school, a longtime fountain pen. This watch had a plain steel band and plain white face, the picture of utilitarianism. It made me think of her. It made me a little sad.

The hands on the watch said I had another ten minutes until the next bus would arrive. The bus service on this line ran every twenty minutes, waiting for no one a minute past the schedule. A shocking realization for me at first—to read the schedule and find that the buses actually would be there at nine-twenty if they said they would be; at home, no such thing had ever happened in the government bus service. As far as I had known, buses arrived and departed when their drivers felt like it, end of story. Schedules, if they existed, were mere suggestions, rather than rules. Like the majority of people, I took a kind of minibus we called a maxi-taxi, and those ran whenever they liked, any time of day or night.

But here, the bus drivers were always on-time, serious professionals, saying *goodmorningma'am* or *goodeveningsir* or whatever to every single person who came in. Miraculously, they asked nobody how their grandson was doing in school, or how their diabetes—in Trinidad we call it sugar—was treating them, or how their *macomere* was keeping. It didn't matter that I saw the same driver more often than not; their tone didn't change when they said *goodmorningmiss* every single morning and *goodafternoonmiss* every single evening.

Standing in the windbreak, I could see the boyish-looking cop staring at me still, and even though I turned away to look in the other direction, I had a feeling he would soon amble my way to make small talk. So said, so done, and he came over, swinging his arms and rhythmically catching his fists together in front as he did. I could feel my heart miss a beat with nervous fear. The gray and yellow of his uniform was different from what I expected of a policeman's; the jaunty yellow stripe was, I felt, unnecessarily frivolous, like a party hat on a pig. In my country the police are not friendly. They do not stop to chat or *old talk* with anybody, especially teenage girls. My anxiety rocketed with his every step.

"So, what brings you to Edmonton? Are you visiting or do you live here?"

Was he going to arrest me for truancy? Was he going to search me for drugs? Would he try to deport me as an illegal alien, even though I had my tourist visa? I started to sweat again, the silk lining of my coat sticking to my sweaty palms. I was terrified he was going to ask to see my passport. Oh, the crap that ran through my head. *Man,* I thought again, *having a panic disorder sucks.*

"Visiting," I squeaked. "Just seeing my aunts."

"Oh? A holiday before you start college, huh?"

"College?" I snapped my head around to look him in the eye despite my agitation and blurted, "I'm only fourteen!"

I could see him take a mental step back as his eyes opened wide and his cheeks grew bright pink. "Uh, I need to check in with my partner. You get home safely, eh?" He quickly ambled back to the other cop. I didn't know what had happened, or why. I already found humans a mysterious species and I was an expert at saying the wrong thing in any situation. Ordinarily the idea that I'd said the wrong thing to a policeman, of all people, would leave me rigid with panic. But suddenly, I was too exhausted from the panic attack I was already having to notice anything but relief that he was gone. I stood alone at the familiar bus stop, my pounding heart slowing its race.

One of the purring buses in the small bullpen of the station suddenly emitted a little burst of wind, a sharp mechanical fart, and rumbled awake. It drove up and I anxiously checked my schedule once more. I was at the right queue. When the bus reached me the door opened with a gasp. The number was written plain as day on the front, and I recognized the driver. Still, I got on and asked him, "Is this the Eighteen?"

"Yup, goodafternoonmiss," he said, nodding his familiar head with an impersonal smile. I paid the fare, lurched to a seat in the middle of the bus, and sat down gratefully on the cold, slippery vinyl. Another mechanical breaking of wind and we were off.

I counted the streets again, and then I was home. Not home home, I thought with a little wave of longing. Was this what tabanca was like? I'd never been in love before, much less lovesick. But I pushed the thought down. I'd worry about it later. Home at Jillian and Julie's house was good enough for now. I reached up, pulled the stop cord, and got out when the bus rolled to a halt. The stop was a half-block from the house, but it was close enough that I hardly had to think about where I was anymore. My anxieties drove off with the bus, for now. I felt immediate relief. My brain switched back on again. And finally, the penny dropped: the boyish cop had been flirting with me before he heard my age.

journal session 1

Dr. Khan made me start this journal after I met with him for the first time. He said, "Write about who you are. Be honest. What's behind that pretty face?"

Honestly? I've never thought of myself as pretty. As a kid I was not the one you'd look at and say, "Oh, what a little angel!" or anything like that. My little face in baby pictures was too serious, and I grew up to be the kind of child adults admire because I am smart and well-read, rather than because of how I look. I am tall and skinny, with dark brown skin and big black eyes that Akilah says make me look older than I am. Though I am shy, I have a good vocabulary, and when I used big words, like I normally did, adults acted like it was a trick I could do, as if I were some kind of monkey dancing on a chain or a dog doing flips on command.

Adults always said to each other: She's so articulate! They would say it right over my head, as if I wasn't even in the room.

And really, sometimes I wasn't. It came to be that I didn't really care what they said anymore. I was doing my thing, talking or writing or reading or whatever, and they would be admiring me like I was a fish in a bowl. And I didn't care, I just swam around in my dirty water and sucked up the stale food and my own pee—metaphorically speaking, of course—and everything was cool. Only, everything wasn't cool.

I was really, really unhappy, like I had this big hole in my belly between my heart and my stomach and I couldn't fill it with food or with TV or books or anything and I just felt sad, all the time, all the time, all the time.

I must have always been that way. I remember that when I was really small, maybe like five or six years old, I picked up a knife to stab my mother after she scolded me for some reason or the other. She denies this story, by the way. She says it never happened. But I remember the weight of the blade in my hand. I remember the rage and pain I felt because she had made me angry, and I re-member thinking if I could hit her hard hard hard she would stop hurting me. And I remember too that she took the knife away and spanked me before I was sent to bed. I woke up later feeling, not for the first time and not for the last, that big pit.

The hole was bigger than me, sometimes, and when I woke up that day, the day after I tried to stab my mother, the hole was there, big and yawning and evil and hard and ugly. I hated myself for what I had done and I wished I had tried to kill myself with that big shiny knife instead of my mother.

It was just one of the things that weighed on me all the time, one of the things that made me feel I wasn't good enough. School was another.

When I was home home I went to an ordinary school. Just like the thousand-and-something other kids at my school, I wore a uniform that was ugly and designed to make me feel unimportant and sheeplike; no individuality allowed. My school wasn't especially big, or special, just a district school with ordinary teachers teaching ordinary subjects like English and maths and social studies and stuff like that.

Akilah and I had been friends from the first day of kindergarten. We were the brightest kids in every class. Everybody thought we'd both go from primary school to secondary school together. But we didn't. When we both sat that Secondary Entrance Assessment, only one of us did well. Akilah went to a prestigious convent school where they taught French, not just English and Spanish. They taught Add-Maths. They won national scholarships. They didn't teach technical drawing or woodwork or clothing and textiles, no practical trades at all; it wasn't that kind of school. Mine was exactly the opposite.

I was bored most of the time. Every year was the same thing. I'd read the books twice before the start of the term, and knew all the information and more because I went to the little library in town with my mother after school and looked up everything I wanted to know before it could come up in school. I read about women's rights, the Black Power movement, the Renaissance, the Harlem Renaissance . . . you name it, I've read it. The librarians smiled benignly at me every time I walked into the library with a stack of books fatter than I was myself. I was all they dreamed of: a bookish girl who would sit quietly, and methodically read the titles they had on the fiction shelves and then start working through the Dewey decimal system of nonfiction. It was a very small library, though, and it didn't take me long to make my way through every book I was even vaguely interested in.

Everybody thought I was smart.

Everybody, except me.

Though I had read all this stuff I wasn't conscious that I knew anything, and I'd always thought of myself as kind of stupid. It didn't help that I had an anxiety disorder that made me freak out every time I took a test. Like the numbers on the buses, everything I knew flew right out of my head when I got anxious. Anxiety started as a little scared butterfly in the pit of my stomach and eventually grew into a giant, sweeping moth that destroyed my ability to focus and recall what I knew. I couldn't tell you how many times I'd failed exams about things I could recite backward and forward.

The last test I sat at my old school was about earth science. I knew all about clouds and fronts and the tides—but not one useful fact stayed in my head during that test. Of course, I failed. I thought back to that test and kicked myself because I knew all the answers. Somehow I couldn't convince my brain that I did, not when the test was actually going on.

Honestly, I don't understand why this stuff happened to me. Why couldn't I just take a stupid test? Why did I feel so bad, ugly, and stupid all the time? Why was everything about me just . . . wrong?

Take for instance my hair. For most of my life I wore my hair in short plaits, which my mother impatiently put in and took out on alternate weekends, averaging about three hours each time she did them fresh. My hair wasn't long enough to reach my shoulders, and in my country that's saying something. Mom always says a woman's hair is her glory and if she has good grass growing up there, it's an asset. I never did see the point. So what if some dead cuticle pushes out longer rather than shorter? Who cares? A few months ago I cut it all off, without consulting my mother, and she hit the roof. But I liked it better that way, almost clinging to my head, so short. *You look like a boy,* my mother said, but I didn't care. It was my hair, and if I wanted to cut it right off I would. I'd never missed it, not even when the cold Edmonton breeze kissed my scalp under my new shorter cut.

I tried to remind her that Aunt Jillian had short hair. Now, understand that my mother is as black as the ace of spades, just like me. For her to change color is pretty tough. But she did it; I swear she turned pale. *Aunt Jillian isn't someone you should take pattern from,* she said, then clammed up and wouldn't say anything else.

I wanted to know why not. All my life she had pointed to her sister, Jillian, as a shining example of virtuous daughterhood, the one who had done good and made their sick mother proud before Granny died. Aunt Jillian was a Canadian citizen, someone with a house and a good job and a wonderful, perfect life in the land of milk and honey—or at least the land of nondairy creamer and NutraSweet. Aunt Jillian was the reason I had to do well in school, because I had to go to the same prestigious high school and meet all the same targets she had to carry on the family legacy. My mom had not been great at school. But I was supposed to be a top student, like Aunt Jillian, be president of the French club, become a swimming champ, lead the debate team, etc., etc. I was supposed to be everything my mother had never had the chance to be, everything Jillian had been so effortlessly.

And then, all of a sudden, Jillian was not someone to take pattern from?

Now, understand that at that point I'd met Jillian once in my life. I was six when my grandmother died of breast cancer and Jillian flew in from Canada for the funeral. She stayed to visit for three weeks. I would never forget her sweetly fragrant suitcases full of clothes and shoes and other presents for my mother and me. The schoolgirl I knew from the faded pictures in my mother's dog-eared photo album had grown up. She was a big woman with a head of short, curly, natural hair. Aunt Jillian wasn't married; my mom said loudly to anyone who asked that Jillian wasn't in the market for a man and would never be. The Jillian I met wore lots of shiny silver jewelry, from the lobes of her ears to the tops, around her neck and on her wrists and her fingers, and even in her nose. She never wore makeup and she was always in black jeans and a black T-shirt, no matter what the weather. She even wore that with a black jacket to Granny Rose's funeral. Of course I asked her, in front of a group of old people and my mortified mother, "Aunty Jillian, didn't you wear those same clothes yesterday?" My mom pinched me hard, but Jillian only laughed and laughed. I never forgot what she said: "Girl, I wear T-shirts and jeans like a uniform. I work too hard at everything else to work at style, too." At six years old I accepted the explanation. And as I got older, if I ever gave Jillian a thought, it was *People can be different, right?*

Of course, when you're a child and your island is the world and your world doesn't include a sophisticated understanding of the real world in its entirety, none of that means anything to you. It was only when I got to Canada and moved into her house that I understood.

Aunty Jillian wasn't single.

Aunty Jillian was gay.

When you're little there's a lot you take for granted. Then, I never really thought about my mother or her family. Now, I had too many other things to worry about than the family I'd never had. My grandfather died before I was born, and I barely got to know Granny Rose. We never visited any distant cousins. It was just my mom, Cynthia, and her big sister, Jillian, who was not really a part of our day-to-day lives because she lived in Canada and she and my mom weren't all that close anymore. Yeah, they were Facebook friends, but I really hadn't paid her that much attention. Was I completely oblivious to the fact that she was obviously, visibly queer? Pretty much. What can I say? It didn't matter to me, not before I moved here to Edmonton.

At least Cynthia had a sister who she grew up with. I grew up alone. And though it sounds strange to say because I am an only child, I have never been my mother's favorite. I felt she had a quiet contempt for everything about me. My hair was only one of the problems. It's actually funny because there's nobody in the world I resemble more than my mother. We have such similar faces, we could pass for sisters. We're both slender and dark, with the same thick, kinky hair, which she wears dead straight. She's shorter than me, though. I guess I got my height from my dad—my mother never talked about him, and I confess I didn't have too much interest in the guy who abandoned us before I was born. Jerk.

What's really weird is that my whole life my mother compared me to Jillian. It happened all the time. If I picked up a book that Jillian might have liked, my mother commented on it. When I wanted to go to the convent school after sitting my Secondary Entrance Assessment, Mom brought up the fact that it was where Jillian had gone—as if I could forget given the photos I'd seen all my life of Jillian so proud in her convent uniform. And when I failed the exam—or rather, failed to pass for the convent school—my mother never stopped mentioning it. She constantly talked about Jillian's accomplishments, her likes and her dislikes, what she used to do as a child, what she used to say, what Jillian used to look like before she cut off her wild, curly hair. Somehow she never mentioned that Jillian was not just gay, but practically married to a woman named Julie.

All that is confusing to me.

For a ton of reasons.

But I've filled my five pages for the day, so I guess I'll write more later.

CHAPTER
TWO

I knocked on the back door before I slipped my key into the lock, just being polite as my mother had taught me to be. After all, this wasn't my house, even if it was my home at the moment. As usual, nobody answered. Jillian and Julie were down in the basement at work.

They were trying to branch out their little web design company into ebook publishing. I didn't know anything about ebooks—nobody I knew in Trinidad read them. We preferred *maco*ing people on Facebook. I wondered if an ebook was the same as publishing your stories online. You could find some decent stories on the internet, like one I had read earlier that day at the library about a girl who fell in love with her neighbor and when their parents found out and broke them up, she tried to kill herself. I liked the writing, but I couldn't believe the girl actually told her mother when she first felt suicidal. Who even does that? I never told any adults that I was sad all the time and that I would rather put an end to those feelings entirely. Who does that? Adults don't think kids are real people anyway. My mother only paid attention to me after I started vomiting my guts out on her kitchen floor. I had no plans to do that on Aunt Jillian's kitchen floor for now.

I liked Aunt Jillian, and the web design stuff was mad decent, though quite frankly I don't care to know how the internet actually works, only that it does. Or I used to care. I used to have email for school, and Instagram like the other kids at my school—how else do you talk to anybody?—but when I had my troubles, as my mother refers to my recent past, I deleted all my accounts. Having Akilah on Skype was my one lifeline. Kind of extreme, but the doctor recommended I stay off social media. Maybe I never will turn them back on. I'm a Caribbean hermit in exile in Edmonton. I could disappear amidst the cookie-cutter houses.

When no one answered my knock, I went into the house. Their kitchen floor, like everything else in Jillian and Julie's house, was spotless. Julie was a fiend for cleaning, Saturdays she'd attack dirt like she had a personal vendetta against it. She would maintain a low-grade surveillance on grime, and there would be occasional sniper fire at it for the rest of the week. My mom was a good housekeeper, but next to Julie she seemed slovenly. There was dust on our bookshelves at home! Not here. Julie even took a cloth and wiped the books themselves. The kitchen was her special domain, and it always smelled a little of pine cleaner. I'd never seen a bread crumb or juice stain on the counters, and a glass didn't get the chance to sit in the sink for more than a minute or two before

Julie swept in to wash up. That was the case this evening. From the bottle they always kept in the fridge I poured myself a glass of cranberry juice, drank it in thirsty gulps, and put the glass in the sink. I went to my room to put down my backpack and the books I had borrowed at the library, and by the time I came back the glass was washed and turned over on the drip tray. There was no sign of Julie herself, though.

"Thanks, Julie!" I yelled from the top of the basement stairs. "I would have washed it, you know!"

"I know, sweetie!" she yelled back. In a second, I heard Aunt Jillian's heavy footsteps on the wooden stairs. Unlike my mother, who made me feel bad for feeling sad, Jillian and Julie acted like I was a regular girl. It was an unusual sensation, being thought of as normal, but a good one. It made me almost happy.

"Hey, sugar," she said as her short fluffy Afro popped into view. "What's up?"

"Oh, nothing much. A cop tried to hit on me at the bus stop," I said, pretending to be casual, though talking about it reminded me of my panic attack—which I didn't mention to Jillian. Instead of telling her I was struggling, and why, I continued with arguably the least important thing that had happened to me that afternoon. "He backed off in a hurry when I told him I was fourteen."

"Almost fifteen," Jillian murmured automatically.

"But still fourteen for now," I replied, winking. "Poor guy."

"Did you tell him that your aunt would kill him too?" Jillian asked drily.

"Oh, no, we didn't get that well acquainted."

"Really," she said, pouring herself some juice. "What did you do today? Go to the gym?" She peered at my sneakers, which were starting to look a hot mess. The laces—let's say they used to be white; and the soles were decidedly un-perky. I worked out on the treadmill at the gym every couple of days on top of regularly walking all over the city and through the suburbs. It was enough to take a toll on my footwear.

"Looks like we need to take you to the mall for some runners," she surmised.

I waved away her suggestion. "Nah," I said, scuffing my toe in embarrassment. With Jillian having paid for my plane ticket already because my mom didn't make that much money, I didn't want her to feel I was taking advantage of her generosity. She was always getting me stuff, little things like music on iTunes and cute notebooks and pens and T-shirts, and I couldn't say no if I wanted to. So I didn't. When I'd gotten to Edmonton, she'd taken me shopping, and now, for the first time in my life, I had a wardrobe of clothes that wasn't just soulless gray uniforms, and that I actually liked. A pair of sneakers would be just one more thing she got me, but I didn't want to ask for them. Looking at my watch, I thought again of how Cynthia never gave me gifts for no reason. It made me feel a squishy discomfort in my belly when I thought of the contrast.

"Could you call them sneakers like a normal person, please?" I begged Jillian with my hands clasped, like it was a really huge deal that she was using a Canadian word. It was a tactic to change the subject. She didn't bite, only watched me cut eye and sucked her teeth with a *steups*. I folded my arms sulkily. "Yeah, maybe I do need new sneakers. But I'm not going to call them runners."

Jillian rolled her eyes. "Whatever, *doux doux*. We were going to go out to dinner anyway; we could stop at the mall on the way there." I didn't have time to react to the ominous feeling in my stomach at the mention of the mall. She took a sip of her juice and broke into a grin, shouting, "Guess what!"

"What?"

"We got our first contract to publish an ebook!"

"Yay, I gather?" I half-smiled.

"Yay, definitely," she confirmed. "It's just one, but it's a start. A writer in California saw our ad on an #ownvoices publishing Facebook page and messaged us. She said she was glad to give her business to a fellow lesbian."

I squirmed a little bit when she said that word. I had been living with her and Julie for a couple of months and obviously I knew that they were gay, but it wasn't something I was comfortable talking about with them. They were amused and sometimes exasperated by my attitude but didn't let it change the way they behaved, either toward each other or toward me. They were active members of the #ownvoices and LGBTQ communities, and I did realize enough to know LGBTQ meant "lesbian, gay, bisexual, transgender, and queer," which, if you think about it, is a bunch of very different kinds of people, but still people who think they have more in common with each other than they have with the rest of the world.

At home home, I'd never given much thought at all to that community, especially as my mother never once said anything about it to me, not even while describing her own sister. Nothing prepared me to consider this topic. Or talk about it.

Frankly, unless you were personally acquainted with someone who identified in that way, odds were you didn't know anything about their world. We didn't have TV shows that showed how Trini LGBTQ people lived their lives, or cute Facebook videos about their families. Aside from Aunt Jillian, there was only one other person everyone knew. She was a trans woman famous for having her surgery because she was the first Trini to do it, I guess. She was on the news a lot and even ran for a city council seat in San Fernando, which she lost. But her visibility was the exception. Where I was from, anybody on the street who looked even a little bit less than straight could get harassed and threatened. The priest at home once stood on the pulpit and preached about the perils of "the sinful LGBTQ lifestyle." Even my school principal brought in police officers to a special assembly to tell us that being gay, lesbian, or anywhere on the spectrum that wasn't heterosexual was against the law, after a boy got beat up because the kids said he was a *bullerman*. I knew that was a nasty word, like if I were to be called nigger. It actually was technically against the law in Trinidad to be gay.

I was straight. At least, I thought I was straight. I had never tested the hypothesis, never having had a boyfriend, but I figured I'd never wanted to have a girlfriend either, so that settled that. Or to be somebody else's boyfriend, come to think of it. The trans woman everybody knew about in Trinidad used to be a guy, obviously. To be honest, that was pretty weird to me. But I didn't know what it was like to be trapped inside the wrong body, which is how some of these people said they felt when they talked about it on their Insta or whatever. Or maybe I did, in a way. Maybe I was not who I was supposed to be and that was why I was so sad all the time.

One day, I would talk to Aunt Jillian about what it was like to be a lesbian. I promised myself. Maybe. But for now, it was okay for us to just sip cranberry juice in the kitchen and look at the bright evening outside the window.

Julie came upstairs and gave me a belly noogie through my T-shirt. I didn't care about wrinkling this shirt. I had on a white one with a frog wearing a crown. There was a speech bubble above him that said "Any day now, princess." I knew it was really a guy's T-shirt, but I thought it was so funny at the time that Julie bought it for me at the freakishly ginormous mall on my first mall trip, when she and Jillian took me on a shopping spree for new clothes. Guy clothes and girl clothes didn't mean that much to me, mostly. I wasn't really into fashion—not the look of an average teenage girl, anyway—especially since I'd cut off all my hair. I just wore whatever I wanted. People said I dressed like Jaden Smith. Needless to say, that just pissed my mother off even more; Jaden Smith is a boy.

"Why don't you at least try to look normal?" my mother used to ask me.

There really wasn't an answer to that, was there? And if we were to go to the mall again, I wasn't going to be changing my habits. Maybe I'd find another frog T-shirt, this time with a prince.

Julie mussed my cropped hair and pecked Jillian on the cheek as she came into the room. "What's happening?"

"I think this one needs new runners," Jillian said, throwing me a teasing look; I faked a shudder and rolled my eyes, mouthing out the word "sneakers" with gusto. After my panic attacks I was often exhausted, but sometimes I acted goofy instead, wired and jittery, like now. Maybe it was another form of nerves. She talked over my head. "I was thinking we could stop at the mall on the way to dinner."

Julie nodded, wiping imaginary dirt from the kitchen counter.

"By the way, Mexican or Italian for dinner?" Jillian asked her.

"I don't care. What do you think, kid?" Julie looked to me.

As usual, I had no idea. "Mexican is nice. But Italian is nice, too. And, come to think of it, so is steak," I stumbled.

"Steak is another option," Jillian agreed. "Mmm . . . red meat." She literally licked her lips. We all laughed.

"You know what they keep saying about how it's full of cholesterol and hormones and it's really, really bad for you?" I teased. They ate steak a couple of times a week, but they still seemed pretty healthy. Then again, they weren't really that old, only about thirty or so. Julie was a little bit older than Jillian, not that she looked it.

"One steak will not kill us, surely?" asked Julie rhetorically with a fake look of horror. Julie's black eyes shined bright with withheld laughter and she reminded me of a pixie, tiny and pretty, despite her usual jeans-and-T-shirt look. Unlike Jillian, though, she sometimes wore saris and kurtas, a kind of long-sleeved man's tunic with buttons at the neck and slits up the sides. I recognized the different styles because I had done a project on Indo-Trinidadian traditions.

Indo-Trinidadians were the largest ethnic group in Trinidad and lots of Trini Indian people wore traditional clothes, beyond just for celebrating religious festivals like Diwali and Eid. People wore them on the regular, especially Trinidadians whose grand-parents and great-great-great-grandparents came from India to work during Indentureship a hundred years ago.

Julie had about a dozen kurtas in different colors, and she wore them in place of a business suit when she had anything of-ficial or important to do, which would remind me of home home. In stark contrast to Jillian's version of dressing up—a blazer over her signature T-shirt and jeans—Julie wore saris, and that got to me more. With her hair long and straight, way past her waist, Julie looked even more like an Indian film star, like Preeti Jhangiani or another actress from the Bollywood billboards on the highway close to my mom's house

Now she swept up her hair into a bun as she walked out of the kitchen toward her bedroom. "You gals make up your minds and I'll be in the shower while you do it."

It was still bright outside as Jillian and I leaned against the kitchen counter, relaxing. I felt so comfortable, even in spite of the terror the outside world had made me feel just a little while earlier. But I still wasn't used to how long it took to get dark here. Home home it got dark by six, earlier if it was a rainy day. The sun came up around six every morning, all year long, and went down quickly around six every evening, all year long. When the sun rose at five in the morning and set at six-thirty at night, that was an extreme. Here in Canada, the sun could come up at six in the morning and go down at nine at night, after hours of twilight. At almost six o'clock, there were still a good three hours of light left. I knew that by the time we were all ready to leave for dinner it would be hours from sunset but already what I thought of as night. It was, to me, entirely magical and a bit astounding. I would never get used to eating dinner in the daylight, I thought.

Eating dinner out was a whole thing in and of itself, though. I'd been to what I'd call a Fancy Restaurant twice in my life before coming to Edmonton. Once was when Jillian visited when I was small, and I barely remember it. The other time was supposed to be a celebration dinner after I finished my Secondary Entrance Assessment. I only have vague, unpleasant memories of not knowing what to do with the cloth napkin, which we never used at home, and having a small meltdown over the long long long menu. I chose a burger, because it was the first thing listed, and my mother was disappointed that I wasn't trying something better. "It's supposed to be a treat," she had hissed at me over the table. I did not arrive in Canada with good memories of going to dinner, and every time I did it with Jillian and Julie I felt a zing of worry that it would be scary and awful. That I would mess something up.

"Thinking about doing another barbecue next Saturday," Jillian said casually. "What you think?"

I grunted. Inside, my heart lurched, switching the focus off the immediate minor threat to the looming Extinction Level Event disaster. A barbecue would mean about twenty people in and out of the house over the course of two days, since guests would come on Saturday and a few wouldn't leave until Sunday. I had made it through a couple of her barbecues before. Some of the people tried to talk to me—and that was just too frightening. I came out of my room to eat and to use the bathroom and to show my face, to be polite, but that was it. I couldn't do sociable. Socializing with strangers made me feel the big, yawning hole in my belly worse than ever, a feeling that no pill had yet entirely controlled.

I didn't tell Jillian any of that, but she must have guessed something like it, because she said, "Hey, I won't pressure you to come out and lime, if you're not ready to hang with our friends. But Stevie says we should be as normal as possible and give you support to help you get through it."

Stevie was Dr. Khan to me. He was my shrink. He was the one making me write a therapy journal. I usually saw him at his office in the city, but Jillian knew him socially; he was involved with the LGBTQ community; that's how she had met him and asked him to take my case when I came. He was a round, brown Indian guy with gentle mannerisms. I liked him, maybe.

"I know," I said, irrationally a little worried that she would feel I was trying to interfere with her life. I was aware she and Julie had considerably reduced their entertaining, one, because they had an extra mouth to feed and it was cutting into their budget, and two, because it was hard for them to ignore how withdrawn and uncomfortable I became when they had company. I fidgeted with my hands for a moment, then said, "It will be fine, Aunty. I'll survive."

She looked at me with concern, her eyes soft. I smiled awkwardly. When we heard the spray of the shower in Jillian and Julie's bathroom, I pushed myself off the kitchen counter. "What should I wear? To dinner, I mean," I asked Jillian, heading to the other bathroom to start my own preparations for going out.

"Just wear what you like, kiddo," she said unhelpfully. I had about an hour until we left. I would need every second of it.

I peered into the closet, trying to decide which of my outfits would be the least offensive. I'd never had so many new clothes at once. Clothes in Trinidad could be expensive, and my single mom wasn't rich. I came with some of my own stuff, but most of the wardrobe I was currently looking at was thanks to Jillian and Julie. The three of us barreled through the mall shops and walked out with bags and bags. I felt like a girl in a rom-com when I wasn't absolutely freaked out about all the choices Jillian and Julie pushed me to make that day in a huge, crowded, loud, scary new place.

The burbling ringtone started up on my phone. It was Akilah on Skype again. She was out of her church clothes and back at home. I recognized her bedroom, the concrete wall with breeze blocks at the top to let the air circulate from outside. Her parents weren't rich either. One of the things we had in common.

"You survived?" She was such a caring friend.

"Yeah, thanks," I said with a sigh, and perched on the bed. "Sorry to be such a pain."

"You're not a pain. That's what friends are for," she said. She was smiling. I was relieved. But my relief was soon replaced by growing terror about the evening to come.

"Ki-ki, we're about to eat dinner. What should I wear?" I groaned in frustration.

"Since when do you care what you wear?" she answered, chuckling. We both knew I was rather offhand about my appearance.

"We're going out to dinner," I said with a moan.

"Again? Your aunty rich or what?" Akilah asked seriously.

"Nah. Food over here so cheap, Ki-ki," I said incredulously. "If you see the fridge! Packed with food. I'll show you. Next time. Now, can you please help me figure out what to put on?" The question came out as a wail. "All I ever wear is jeans and a T-shirt. Jillian does it and it looks cool. I do it and I look like a hobo. I feel my Aunty Julie would appreciate my trying on something different for a change. Like a dress or something."

"I haven't seen you in a dress since First Communion," Akilah teased. "Besides, you look good in jeans and a T-shirt. Make that booty pop," she said. I looked at her wide grin on the screen, trying to read whether she was being serious or not.

"Leave my booty out of it," I murmured.

"What kind of Trinidadian woman are you, if you don't care about your butt?" Now she was laughing outright. "We sing songs about it, even! 'Sugar bum, sugar bum-bum,' " she sang.

The lyrics to a famous calypso didn't impress me. "Blah, blah, blah," I answered. Out of the blue, I thought of the pig in the party hat at the bus station. I asked her, "Ki-ki? Do you think I'm pretty?"

She was quiet for a long moment. "I've told you. Yeah, sometimes."

"Wow, that's a ringing endorsement." My shoulders slumped, and my disappointment must have been clear from my tone.

"No, that's not what I mean," she said. "You have a really pretty face and a nice figure, but you hide yourself away in baggy, shapeless clothes like you're afraid someone will notice you're beautiful. That's why I said 'sometimes.' What I should have said is you're always pretty but sometimes you don't let it show. It's like you're scared of people finding you attractive."

"Meh, shut up." I scowled but I knew she was right. I had major hang-ups about the way I looked. "You know that every Trinidadian boy only wants a red-skinned girlfriend with long, curly hair and a big butt. Brown-skinned girls are okay, but their lips and noses can't be too African—"

"Boys are dumb."

"Yeah, but I'm too dark, my hair is too picky, and worst of all, my butt is flat! I'll never get a boyfriend," I bawled in mock agony.

"Papa! I never knew you wanted a boyfriend," Akilah teased. "You always have your head stuck in a book. Boys at your school don't even know you exist."

A truthful girl, Akilah. Which was neither here nor there at the moment; the point was that she went to an all-girls school, so how would she know what anyone at my coed institution thought of me? "What would a convent girl like you know about boys at my school, anyway?" I grumbled, picking at an old scab. It still killed me that Akilah—who always aced her exams—had been placed in the very prestigious school I had dreamed of attending, while I had been placed in an ordinary one. All because of that one exam.

"I saw that girl we went to primary school with, the one who's in your class—what's her name? Britney? She was at the mall. You might think nobody talks your business but she said your whole school is full of rumors about why you left so suddenly before the end of the school year. The talk is that you got pregnant and your mother sent you away—except that nobody can figure out who the baby daddy was that knocked you up. They think you have never been alone with a boy in your life."

"Who's this 'they' and why do 'they' maco so much? I had an immaculate conception, then?" I giggled, but I was nauseated. Not for blasphemy; I went to church with my mom, yeah, but I was not at all religious. Of course, "they," whoever they were, were right. I never had been alone with a boy. To be honest, I wouldn't have known what to do if someone found me interesting. And the thought that anybody was talking about me made me a little sick. I much preferred to be invisible. But I put those thoughts behind me. "Ki-ki, back to my IRL problems. What am I going to wear?"

"All right," she said, flexing her arms and swinging her fists like a boxer warming up for a fight. "What do we have to choose from?"

I panned the camera to show the contents of the small closet lit by a dim overhead bulb. Bright red plaid flannel caught my eye. "What about this?" I pulled out the long-sleeved shirt and put it on to show Akilah.

"With what?"

"Dunno."

She pursed her lips and tapped them with her index finger thoughtfully. "I know. What about that little green thing you showed me the other day?"

"With the crossbones on it? Okay. With which jeans?" I'd already pulled out three different washes and tossed them on the bed. I rummaged in the dresser drawer where I kept my T-shirts and selected the baggy crop top she'd recommended. I put it next to the black, the indigo, and the faded blue. "Yasssss," Akilah squealed.

"Boyfriend jeans for the win!" I shouted giddily. I could not forget that I was getting dressed to go shopping and to dinner, both of which would make my anxiety shoot through the roof. Yet I felt so happy in that moment. My best friend and I were laughing together and planning outfits like normal girls. Aunty Jillian and Aunty Julie were the coolest foster parents in the world. It was just a brief excursion. What could go wrong?

journal session 2

"Write about your mom," he said. "It will *help*," he said.

If my mom and I were in a Facebook relationship our status would be "It's Complicated." My mom calls regularly. That is both a good thing and a bad thing.

I know it might not sound like it, but I love my mom. She gave me life and I owe her my eyes and my good cheekbones and my long legs and my razor-sharp wit and my love of reading. We have the same skin color, and my hair is like hers—or would have been if she didn't straighten it with chemicals every two months. But despite our similarities, I've always been a huge disappointment to her. I looked into her eyes and saw the shadowed hopes that one day I'd turn into the kind of girl she wanted: a nice, sweet, kind girl who wears dresses constantly and goes to parties and has lots of friends and went to a prestigious school and did well in all the suitable subjects. What she ended up with was me.

I knew that every time she looked at me, she saw all the things I could have been but—as she put it—I chose not to be. I was a walking failure to her.

And that was before I was rushed to the hospital.

Because I am an only child, there is not even a sibling to take the pressure off me. My mom has Aunty Jillian to compare herself to for all her life—and that must be terrible, since Jillian was perfect, except for the teeny, tiny fact that she was a homosexual—a cardinal sin in the eyes of our Trinidad community. Worse yet, my mom is the cheap knockoff version of Jillian. Younger by two years, she doesn't consider herself as pretty, as smart, nor as ambitious. Jillian left Trinidad at twenty to study in Canada and never moved back home home. By Canadian standards she isn't a great success, just average, but by island standards anything one does "away" is made that much more special and exciting and extraordinary. My mom, on the other hand, became a primary school clerk after my Granny Rose died. Being a clerk was a job Cynthia could do as a single mother, not a vocation. She has a comfortable, boring life—nothing like Jillian's. As a magazine writer Jillian was always jetting around Canada and the US for stories, getting to meet lots and lots of people. My mom leaves for work at eight in the morning, comes home at five in the afternoon, goes to church on Sundays, and lives a quiet, dull life.

Jillian didn't tell my mom that she had to struggle to do all that jetting around because she didn't have a steady job and she lived hand-to-mouth. "I woke at thirty with no savings, no insurance, and no backup plan for retirement. Thank God for socialism, eh?" Jillian told me ruefully, winking, in one of our first conversations when I got to Canada.

She said she envied my mom's stability. "If she only knew how much I wish I had a kid and a pension. Oy vey!" she said with a laugh. "I'd do anything to know that when I'm sixty I can sit back if I want. Cynthia doesn't know how good she has it."

One of the reasons she and Julie had set up the publishing company was so that they could get more stability. And Jillian had given up her magazine work. They want to start a family. I know this because one night when I was going to the bathroom really late, I overheard them having an argument. I felt like a creep, sneaking as close to their door as I could without being obvious, just to listen. Jillian was crying, saying, "You don't know what it's like to want a baby, Julie, you don't."

Julie's voice was low and sweet, but firm. "I know what it feels like. Come on, you know I want a baby as much as you do. But I don't see how we can have a child together right now!"

I didn't see how either. Same-sex couples were a thing, of course I knew that; I'd seen it on TV and, like, a ton of videos. But I didn't actually know any kids with gay parents. How would it work? I wondered.

Jillian wasn't done, though, and I barely heard her last words through her sobs. "Every time I think of what Cynthia must have put that poor child through . . . Why wasn't she my daughter? Why wasn't she my little girl?"

It didn't make sense how she was talking about me.

I tiptoed back to my bedroom in confusion mixed with an unfamiliar but pleasing feeling. I guess up until that point I had never considered myself such a prize. Imagine that someone wanted me. Me!

I haven't spoken to my aunt about what I overheard, because

45

I don't want her to know I listened to their private conversation, but it's stuck in my mind. It was the first time I realized that someone in my family could want me in their life.

My mother certainly never behaves like that. She doesn't mistreat me. She is a decent mother and I wouldn't call her abusive or anything. I got the normal one or two slaps most Caribbean kids got from their mothers for bad behavior. But neither by word nor deed has she showed she really wants me around. She's done what she had to do. I am a chore, a responsibility, but not a pleasure and certainly not a privilege.

Now that I am in exile, every week, like clockwork, my mom either phones on the landline or Skypes me. She asks the same questions, carefully avoiding any mention of my illness. We don't talk about it anymore, after her first recriminations and attempts to blame me for my craziness. Now she pretends I am on holiday. My troubles have somehow turned into an extended vacay.

CHAPTER
THREE

The first time I went to the West Edmonton Mall I had the overwhelming impression of, well, being overwhelmed. It was huge. It was literally the biggest mall on this continent and was as big as my hometown. It had its own waterpark and ice rink. There was a pirate ship, for crying out loud. Arcades. Amusement parks. A roller coaster. Shops. Shops for shoes, books, clothes, household goods, electronics, teddy bears, jewelry, art, you name it. Of course, we had malls in Trinidad. But this was not a regular mall. You could walk for days and never reach the end. After the Apocalypse, all the survivors in Edmonton could probably just pack up and move into the mall. I had never seen so much stuff in one place.

Jet-lagged and still half dozing from my long trip the day before, I stumbled through dozens of shops behind Jillian and Julie, who were trying to get me to look excited instead of scared. "Try this," they kept saying, as they put items in my hand and walked me to changing room after changing room. Honestly, all I remember is a blur of color and movement. I didn't speak much because I was biting my lips, holding back my panic.

This trip couldn't be as bad—even if walking toward the entrance was like preparing to enter a new country, one that was bright and noisy and full of decisions for me to make. I took a deep breath and exhaled. I felt like that afternoon's misfortune was behind me. I could do this. We were on a clock, too, so Julie took charge and went straight to the first sports-gear place we came to. Jillian followed and my energy abruptly dipped. I trailed behind them, dragging my feet. Inside I was still kind of excited. Who wouldn't want to replace beat-up old sneakers with new kicks? But that was tangled with my shame. Shame that I was completely dependent on my aunt. Shame that I was a strain on her limited resources. Which started me thinking about the reasons I was in Canada in the first place. Which reminded me of my panic attack that afternoon. I felt miserable.

Julie pointed out a few styles on the shelves and I shrugged ambivalently. She was patient, though. "What about this? I think it's a good brand. They look comfortable," she said, picking up a white tennis shoe with glow-in-the-dark pink stripes. A bright orange sticker indicated it was marked down.

I shrugged again. I didn't love them, but they were on sale. Less expense for my aunts. A salesman came over and Julie asked him for my size. We sat on the chairs waiting for him to return with a pair for me to try on. I toed off my shoes and huddled my socked feet together, glued my eyes to the display wall of shelves and shelves of sneakers, and tried to shrink into my oversized plaid shirt and shapeless jeans. Julie checked her phone while we waited.

"Try these," the guy said, coming back holding a box and sitting in front of my chair. He handed me the shoes one at a time.

I eased in my feet. The shoes were comfy. The thick padding inside made my toes and insteps feel as snug as a bug in a rug. Standing, I bounced a little to test the springy soles. The shoes were ugly, but boy, did they fit. I gave Julie two thumbs-up and a brief smile.

"Wow, that was quick! You sure you want these?" In a low voice just for me to hear, she said, "We can try others, you know. Take your time. We don't have to rush."

"No, it's okay, Aunty. I like them. Can we get them?" I was so happy with how fast we got my new, cushy shoes. I didn't want to take them off. I even kept them on while Jillian paid at the register. It wasn't half as horrible as I'd imagined it would be. And we were done shopping for the day. I finally felt relieved as we left the mall.

But only for a moment. Lunch was a distant memory and my belly began to growl as I slid into the backseat of the car. We still had to go to dinner at a Fancy Restaurant.

We walked into Tacos and Tequila—we voted to have Mexican after all—and I nearly died.

A boy who was seated at one of the tables in a corner with two neatly dressed, oldish white men was the most gorgeous guy I'd ever seen. He looked about sixteen, with clear skin the color of an apple about ten minutes after it had been cut, sort of caramel brown but not so buttery. His curly hair was so perfect that it could have been in a shampoo commercial. He had hazel eyes, pink lips, a button nose, and a smattering of reddish-brown freckles on his high cheekbones. I had never seen anybody so good-looking in real life before. I mean, I'd seen movie stars, and they were attractive, but they were only about half my height in real life so I figured there were lots of things that clever camera angles could simulate, including a cute face.

There were no cameras here. Just the best-looking guy I'd ever seen. And he was tall AF, judging by the length of the legs I saw folded under the table and the length of the arms I saw folded above it.

Then Julie and Aunt Jillian caused me to have a minor heart attack in the middle of the restaurant.

"It's Nathan and Bill!" Julie nudged Jillian, pointing to the two men and the demigod of a teenager. "Wow, I haven't seen them in ages! I wonder if they've ordered yet."

We had been walking behind the hostess who had met us at the door. Jillian stopped her and started to explain. "*Sí, por supuesto,* sure," the hostess said with a light Latin Canadian accent, smiling as she gestured for us to go on.

Julie waved and led the way forward. I barely noticed the restaurant, which seemed cheerful and bright with colorfully embroidered white tablecloths and centerpieces of low baskets of fresh flowers. There were hellos, long-time-no-sees, and plenty of air-kisses between the adults while the boy and I nodded at each other awkwardly. After Jillian introduced me to the adults, Julie added, "Nathan and Jillian were friends at university. He and Bill are partners in their own law firm downtown."

"And this young man is Joshua, my son," Nathan said. I could see the resemblance between them. They were both tall and slim. Both had very symmetrical features, bright hazel eyes, and long eyelashes. But while Nathan was a blond white man, Joshua was clearly black. He must have got his adorable nose, those exquisite cheekbones, and his dark, curly hair from his mom's side of the family.

"Joshua is also Jillian's godson, isn't that right, Jillian?"

Jillian nodded. "Though I haven't seen him since he was in grade school! He grow up nice, eh, to use a Trini expression." They all laughed except for Joshua. Was the Cute Boy blushing?

Nathan insisted we join them. They hadn't ordered anything but drinks, and those hadn't been served yet; Nathan hailed the hostess and asked for a new pitcher of margaritas and another table for us. We stood in a quiet group as a waiter brought over an extra table, joining them together to make one long rectangle. After fixing our place settings, three to a side, he dashed away. The hostess reappeared and gave us menus once we'd taken our seats, Jillian and Julie and Nathan on one side, Bill and Joshua and me on the other. Rushing back, the waiter brought margaritas for the adults, with four weirdly wide glasses with salt-encrusted rims. Next he came with glasses of ginger ale with ice for me and Joshua. He ran to the front again and got a pitcher of water, too, pouring some for everyone as the hostess oversaw. In Trinidad we don't tip, not usually; it's just not something we do. But these two people were working so hard, even I, a Trini, had to admit they were earning a nice one tonight.

The adults helped themselves to their drinks in the odd glasses. Out of the corner of my eye, I saw Joshua darting a look at me as he picked up the ginger ale and offered to cheers mine with a shy smile. I didn't want him to see that my hands were trembling. My voice was shaky too when I croaked, "Oh, thanks." My throat was a dune in the Kalahari.

I couldn't believe we were having dinner together, me, next to the most gorgeous boy I'd ever seen in real life. I wished I could call Akilah instantly to discuss the new development of the Cute Boy and the terror I felt, but I knew if I pulled out my phone it would be rude and Jillian and Julie would be disappointed in me. So I ducked my head and tried not to pass out from lack of oxygen.

I should have said steak. It wasn't as messy as Mexican, and between the guacamole, salsa, and tortilla chips there was all kinds of potential for food falling on my clothes, my clothes that I obviously shouldn't have worn. My outfit was cool for the mall, but now there was this guy and we were at dinner and I felt I looked like a slob in ripped, baggy jeans and a flannel shirt. I was so scared I'd make a fool of myself and drop the food like a baby. Oh God, and those hideous sneakers! I should have at least put on some ChapStick. My mouth was dry and my lips felt ashy. I was horribly unprepared for the moment. There was a sour, cramped feeling in the pit of my stomach. Imagining how I must have looked to the Cute Boy, I was filled with self-disgust. I lost my appetite, though minutes before I had been hungry enough to eat my own arm.

Jillian looked at me from time to time while she chatted with Nathan and Bill. She made eye contact with Julie, who turned her attention to us. "So, Joshua!" Julie said, beaming.

He blushed. "People call me Josh," he told her.

"Lovely to meet you, Josh," she said, before adding to Jillian, "This gorgeous kid is your godson?" She asked Josh directly, "Where has Nathan been hiding you?"

"I live in Brooklyn with my mom," Josh said. "I'm with my dad on vacations."

"Oh, so you'll be here for a few more weeks, then?" He nodded. I swallowed, watching a determined expression settle on Julie's face. Something told me she was going to try to get us to be friends. She wouldn't . . . would she? But I was right about the glint in her eye. She pointed to me. "She's here for a while, too. Maybe you two can spend some time together," Julie suggested. I tried to keep breathing but it was a challenge. My throat still wasn't working that well. I made a grimace that I tried to pass for a smile.

The waiter came back and took our entrée orders. I went last, having the same thing as Julie, chicken mole. I had no idea what it was; I'd never seen Mexican food in Trinidad. But I thought, who doesn't like chicken? The truth was it was easier to order what someone else had, to just avoid choosing from the menu.

"How is your mom, by the way?" Jillian asked Josh. "I haven't seen Shelly in . . . gosh, I don't know how long. Is she still an awesome dancer?"

Nathan jumped in mischievously. "She never was as good a dancer as you, Jillian."

"Ha!" They shared a fond look. My aunt laughed and shook

her head. "Nathan used to run after me back in the days when he thought I was straight," she confided to me across the table in an outrageously loud whisper, much to the Cute Boy's mortification and the other adults' amusement. *Good,* I thought, watching him blush. *At least I'm not the only one who has to suffer through this ordeal of Death by Shame.*

"Can you blame me?" Nathan asked, fake leering at Jillian. "Look at you. What's not to love? Besides, you never told me you were gay back then."

Jillian laughed again. "I never told anyone I was gay back then. Coming out was a process. Besides, Shelly was so much more into you."

"Good thing I married her," Nathan quipped. "Though God knows that didn't go how we planned."

His joke fell flat. A short, uncomfortable silence fell over the table. I guessed Nathan and Shelly had had a rough divorce. The fact that she'd moved to another country afterward was probably a giant clue.

"How do you like Edmonton?" Julie asked Josh, changing the subject.

Before he could say anything, Nathan answered for him while looking squarely at me. "Biracial kids like Joshua have a hard time living in largely white communities like Edmonton." He sounded like he'd read that in a manual. I nodded, choking down a dry tortilla chip I hastily grabbed from the basket in front of me so I wouldn't have to respond.

I personally thought Edmonton was as homogenous as you wanted it to be. I saw plenty of black and brown people in the city when I walked around.

Julie seemed to agree with my thought. "Come on, Nathan. I think you can safely call Edmonton multicultural. Even right here in this restaurant, there is diversity: I was born in Canada but I'm South Asian, Indian to be specific. And Jillian and her niece are black, from Trinidad. The waiter is Indigenous. The hostess is Latin American. And at least two of us at this table are gay, a minority in itself—don't you think that counts as diversity?"

Nathan hemmed and hawed while he tried to figure out how to reply. I could tell he and Bill were work partners, not romantic partners, from the way they talked to one another. For some reason Nathan hadn't hung out with Jillian and Julie for a really long time. As Nathan kept talking, I began to guess why. "Yes, yes, I guess Edmonton has those people. . . ." He waved his hand in a vague, dismissive gesture. I presumed by "those people" he meant gay people, black people, Caribbean people, Asian people, Native Canadians . . . pretty much anyone who wasn't a straight white man. I wasn't crazy, because even Bill began to look at him with a frown. "Yes, there's diversity. But compared to New York? To Toronto, eh? Those people still aren't the ones in power. Look at Edmonton's City Council. Hardly any of those people there."

There was something in his tone that made me ashamed of my skin. It made me feel insignificant, even though he was saying words that should have been inclusive. Instead, I felt invisible. I wondered what he called black people when his son and other people of color weren't around. Josh just sat there with his face turning redder and redder; soon he was the same shade as his freckles.

I didn't say anything. I toyed with my phone, spinning it around and around on the table. The food arrived in record time and I instantly regretted my order when I saw how much sauce there was on the dish. While the adults kept their conversation up, I scraped off the sticky brown goop and cut up my chicken. I dipped the slivers of meat cautiously into the sauce and ate them one at a time. Or tried to. I had never been so hungry but so completely incapable of eating. My anxiety made my mouth arid. Everything took forever to chew, ending up in an pasty, tasteless lump at the back of my tongue. I had to force myself to swallow with a gulp. It was noisy. My ears burned in mortification. There was a fiery ball where my stomach should have been.

But it wasn't all bad. Even though eighty percent of me was freaking out, there was a good twenty percent left. That part of me was focused entirely on Josh. I heard him breathing. I smelled his cologne; it was nice and reminded me of a park or something sunny and fresh. We had plenty of space between us but somehow, I could feel how warm he was from all the way in my seat.

Josh and I kept sneaking peeks at each other when we thought the other wasn't looking, a fact that wasn't lost on Nathan, who thought it was a good idea to draw attention to our glances.

"These two can't keep their eyes off each other, Jill," he chortled.

I thought the restaurant floor should open right up and swallow me whole, but it didn't and I was stuck there, sitting next to the Cute Boy and feeling sicker and sicker. The lumpy food and Nathan's offhand comment stuck in my throat. I started to sweat, which made everything worse because now I was feeling not just badly dressed, but damp, too. As soon as I could, I excused myself and dashed to the bathroom. For a while I leaned my wet forehead against the large, cold mirror, trying to collect myself, trying to ketch mehself, as Trinis would say. I stood back. The mirror was surrounded by tiny sombreros and maracas and chili peppers. The décor here was super cheesy, and at another time I might have laughed about it with Akilah, but it didn't matter to me now. All I felt was my deep shame, and the awful pain in the center of my belly. Looking at myself, all I could see was a skinny, ugly girl in garish, mismatched clothes that didn't fit.

I took ten deep breaths, as Dr. Khan had taught me in our first session when I described what a panic attack felt like. He'd said the breathing should calm me down, but it didn't, not now. I reminded myself that I was in a public restroom and it was no place for a meltdown. I kept repeating in my head, trying to convince myself, *I will not scream, I will not scream, I will not scream.* Somebody was trying to come in, pushing against the door, so I went into one of the three cubicles to hide. Locked in, I went through the mantra again. *I will not scream, I will not scream, I will not scream.*

I reached a shaky hand into my pocket for my phone, but it wasn't there. I must have left it on the table when I fled.

I will not scream, I will not scream.

Nope.

I screamed. I stuffed my fist in my mouth and I screamed and screamed again. It was a little scream, but it burst the dam and I started to cry. I tried my best to muffle the huge, ugly gulps and gasps, pressing my face into my hands to hold in the noise, my tears, and the trailing clear snat that dripped from my nostrils. When the woman in the stall next to mine asked very timidly,

"Are you okay in there?" I quickly got my act together and ceased crying and stopped my hands from shaking and generally tried to sound normal.

"Oh, fine, fine," I said. "Just letting off a little steam." I closed my eyes and felt my sense of hopelessness rising higher and higher. Once again, I wished I had my phone. But even if I had it, should I call Ki-ki and burden her with my crap again, for the second time today? I was a sandbag, dragging down everyone around me. No wonder my mother didn't want me and sent me away. I was worthless all over again. Why was I even alive?

The woman left the bathroom and I stayed where I was for a minute. I put the seat cover down and sat on it, rocking back and forth and squeezing my eyes shut to try to not feel so bad, but nothing was working. My pounding heart felt like it wanted to jump out of my mouth.

It must have been a long minute. Eventually, Julie came in.

"You all right in there, muffin?"

I didn't answer. I couldn't. If I'd tried to, I'd have started bawling really hard. Her soothing voice was the last thing I needed. All it did was remind me of the mom I wished I had. Home home, Cynthia had once or twice found me crying. All she ever said was "You want me to give you something to cry for? Is a good cut-tail you want!"

Instead, Julie said, "Honey?" She sounded concerned. "Open the door. Let me in."

Numbly, I unlocked the stall for her. She took a look at me and hugged me tight and said it'd be okay. That didn't help much, only made me want to cry more, and so I did. I also started hitting my balled fists against my thighs. Something inside me had come undone.

I'm on some pretty strong antidepressants and antianxiety meds, and have been ever since they took me to the hospital after I overdosed on painkillers to try to kill myself.

I remember a group of doctors, quiet as a cloud, drifting from bed to bed in the children's ward. A kind-faced older man seemed to do the talking for the team as he explained my wonky brain chemistry, and said that I might have to take meds for the rest of my life. Nice.

Anyway, the medication isn't the only thing they prescribed. I was also supposed to go to group therapy with a counselor, but my mom couldn't afford to pay a shrink and, since arriving in Canada, I had rejected any suggestion of it when Dr. Khan brought it up. Every now and then my aunts tentatively raised the question but I always changed the subject. I was taking my meds—antidepressant in the morning, antianxiety pill at night. Dr. Khan had made me promise to write in a journal. That was all I could do for now and since I had been in Edmonton it had worked to keep me more or less okay. I had felt panic sometimes, like at the bus stop earlier, but I didn't generally want to tear my own face off; I felt sadness, but not the giant abyss that I had wanted to fall into the day I took the bottle of pills, to fall and never return.

But those good old days of managing my depression and anxiety with just medication seemed to be over. I was having the ice cream sundae of meltdowns in the bathroom of Tacos and Tequila.

After holding me for a few minutes, Julie sat me down, told me not to worry, and left to fetch Aunt Jillian.

Could anything be worse than what I was going to call this—the Tacos and Tequila Incident? As crazy as it seemed, the Cute Boy seemed interested in me. He was looking at me, wasn't he? Yeah, and he knows you were looking at *him*, too. His dad announced it to the whole wide world. I sat on the toilet seat replaying the entire awful episode over and over in slow motion. I groaned from deep down in my cramping belly.

When Aunt Jillian appeared, she didn't even blink to see me wet-faced and shaking in a toilet cubicle. She went into crisis mode. "Right. Let's get her out of here and back home. We'll deal with this better there."

The idea of going out into the restaurant looking like that made me freak out even more. I clutched Jillian's hand. "Please, please, Aunty, please don't make me have to say goodbye," I begged. This time, I wasn't playing or being goofy. I was really scared of having anybody else see me with my *snatty* nose and my still-dripping face swollen from crying.

"Of course you don't have to say goodbye, sweetie. We'll tell them you're not feeling well and you send your apologies, that's all," said Julie. Though I was kind of glad I didn't have to talk to anyone, especially the Cute Boy, somewhere under the weeping, wailing, and gnashing of teeth I was a bit sorry. He really was gorgeous. That was the last coherent thought I had for days.

journal session 3

The last time I felt like that, I had a nervous breakdown. This is what I remember.

I opened my eyes to a white fluorescent strip light. The bed below me was hard and narrow. I tried to turn, feeling the thin sheet sliding on the vinyl mattress cover, and reached out to push myself up. That's when I noticed I was wearing a strange gown and had an IV drip in my arm. I looked around. Five other kids lay in railed beds like mine around the room, mostly sleeping or playing on their phones. One was awake and looking at me. There was a giant yellow banana painted on the wall behind his bed. I guessed it was the children's ward of a hospital. It was day; I could see light through the windows in one wall, but I couldn't tell what time it was. My stomach burned like acid.

I had a sore throat, too. Banana Kid heard me clearing it and took it as an invitation to chat. He asked in a friendly, curious tone, "You's the one who take tablets to kill yourself? I hear the nurses talking about you."

I slumped back down and turned my face away. Luckily, I was in a corner. It was what I deserved, anyway, to lie alone in a corner. I was alive. I didn't know how to feel about that. Should I be disappointed? Or relieved?

"Nursie!" Banana Kid yelled. "Look, the girl who take the tablets wake up!"

Outrageous! You rude little—! I swung around to complain but the words froze in my mouth when I noticed there was a counter by the doorway to the ward where two women in white sat doing paperwork. One of them, a chubby brown-skinned lady, sighed loudly and creaked to her feet. Her lack of amusement showed in her stiff neck. "Shhh! Hush, Clive. You feel because you living here you could bawl out any old way? Have some behavior!" After scolding him in a stage whisper, she said to me in a normal voice, "Missy, how are we this morning?" So it was morning, then. As she waddled toward my bed I shrank back into the hard mattress. She took my arm and checked the IV needle stuck in the bend of it. Clear liquid dripped from the plastic bag hanging on the metal stand, going down a skinny plastic tube into my arm via the needle into my vein. It looked just like on TV, I remember thinking.

"Doctor is on his way," she said. She put a blood pressure cuff around my arm and pushed some buttons. I lost interest and looked back toward the wall as she took my temperature and pulse. The machine beeped, squeezed my arm, beeped again, and relaxed. I didn't watch as she unwrapped the cuff.

I kept my face to the wall until she said, "Why would a nice young girl like you, with so much to live for, try to take your own life? That would be such a loss. You are so beautiful." Her tone was kind and sympathetic. I turned just enough to see her face. She had relaxed and wasn't looking so stiff anymore. There was a spark in her eye. "You know who can help you with those feelings?"

I shook my head. She leaned in. "Jesus can help you, dear heart. Just call his precious name. Jesus . . ." She closed her eyes and started to pray for me right there. I wasn't offended. On the contrary, it was kind of nice to have someone express regret that I might have died. Still, she was a stranger who was also breathing in my face and making presumptions about my spiritual life. How did she know I wasn't already calling on Jesus and Mary and Joseph and a wide variety of saints? I mean, I wasn't. But I could have been. And wasn't it super unprofessional of her to pray with me? I was a patient. I was pretty sure there were rules about that kind of thing. She rambled on for a while, adding a few verses from the Book of Psalms I recognized from church. I was starting to get hungry when the doctor arrived.

A tall, skinny old man strode in at the head of the flock of younger people. He was the only one not wearing a white coat. Instead, he had on a sharp pinstriped suit. He must have been boiling in the heat. The nurse muttered a hurried amen, handed over my medical chart to him, and stood to one side away from the herd.

From my best recollection, I think he had on a purple tie. If he wasn't so old, he'd have been handsome. He had a kind face, and eyes that really saw you, inside. The younger doctors all stared at him in adoration and hung on his every word while he talked about me as though I was still unconscious.

"Take the medical history, Smith," the doctor instructed a junior attendant with buckteeth. Smith, I presumed, timorously asked about a thousand questions about my shots, if I'd had measles, if I'd ever been in hospital or had surgery before. I whispered my responses, keeping them short and to the point. Some questions, like what conditions ran in my family, I couldn't answer. "My mom can tell you," I said. And it hit me all at once that she wasn't there. Panic, pure and hot, started to fill my chest. I think the doctor was a mind reader. He saw my eyes widen and asked the nurse immediately, "Nurse, where is the patient's mother? Wasn't she here overnight?" I think he asked so I would know she hadn't left me there alone, not really.

"Yes, Doctor. She had to go in to work to apply for emergency leave, she said." The nurse was back to her stern professional attitude. I focused on how dotish it seemed that my mother would have to physically go to the school where she worked to ask for emergency leave. Wasn't she having an emergency?

"Call me when she returns. We have a lot to talk about." His eyes were lasers behind his thick, round tortoiseshell-frame glasses. "So." He said nothing else, just looked at me. The junior doctors were like ghosts standing behind him. My hunger vanished, replaced by a jittery feeling. I wanted to cry. I was on the verge of ripping out the IV and making a run for it when he finally spoke again. "No smartphone, I see? Good. Keep it that way. Social media is terrible for you. So, young lady. I understand you took some tablets. Thirty paracetamol. You took them last night? Why?"

I had nothing to say. The tears were quivering behind my lashes now, but they hadn't yet fallen. My world was a tight bubble of rage, pain, and shame. I felt dirty and pointless.

"You know that you could have hurt yourself?" I closed my eyes. Of course I knew. That was the whole point. I would hurt myself until the pain stopped, forever. The tears squeezed out and ran down my cheeks but I didn't answer him. How could I explain the ache I felt inside, the torment that ripped me to pieces when I was alone? I hate myself. I think I deserve to be dead. The world would be a better place without me in it. Yeah, right, I could totally tell him that. He would completely get it.

He waited still.

Stubbornly, I remained silent.

Finally he said kindly, "We will keep you under observation for a few days. The medication you took can cause permanent organ damage, so we'll watch to make sure that didn't happen. I want to talk to you about why you took the tablets. Did you mean to harm yourself?"

There it was. The big question. Crazy girl, were you trying to commit suicide when you swallowed a full bottle of your mother's painkillers? I opened my teary eyes and darted looks at the doctors and the ward behind them. Banana Kid leaned forward in his bed. The nurse raised an eyebrow and pursed her lips. I lay back, closed my eyes, and pretended to go to sleep. When I wouldn't answer any more questions, the doctor talked quietly to the nurse before touching my shoulder. "She's going to give you some medicine," he said, and left. From behind my closed eyelids, I heard him being followed by the cloud of younger doctors. The nurse remained and fiddled with my drip. Then she, too, left me alone and I drifted off.

I woke up again when Cynthia roughly shook me awake. My mouth was gross and my teeth were fuzzy when I yawned. My hunger was gone. I didn't feel panic. I didn't feel much of anything. It was as though I was seeing the world from behind a thick layer of glass. Saying nothing, my mother handed me a toothbrush, tube of toothpaste, and bottle of water. Brushing my teeth was the last thing I wanted to do. But I did it, rinsed my mouth with some of the water, and spit into the pink plastic bedpan she placed in my lap. I wiped my mouth with the back of my hand. All that time, I felt dead inside. What was the point? Didn't I deserve to have filthy teeth and terrible breath? I was a waste of space anyway. Who cared whether all my teeth fell out? Who cared if I was dead? Other than the Christian nurse, that is. I was causing my mother terrible inconvenience. Yet, somewhere deep down, I was relieved she was there, even though her face showed exactly how much patience she had with this new development. Suicide attempt. Great.

Someone had left a bland, flabby cheese sandwich and a lukewarm box of juice on a platter on my bedside table. Mom thrust it at me. I struggled to eat the tasteless bread. Without warning, my mother stood and walked away. The nurse waddled over. "Everything okay, dearie? The sandwich all right?"

"Yes, thank you," I choked out, swallowing painfully. I hoped the nurse wasn't going to pray again. I just wanted her to go away. I grabbed for the juice box and stuck the straw in, immediately sucking up a mouthful of tepid orange juice to avoid saying anything further.

"Mummy went to see Doctor," she said. "He gave you some medication, so he has to explain it to her, what the different tablets are for and how you have to take them. You might have to take some for a long time. Some people take them for their whole lives. You can't drink alcohol with these tablets, missy, don't forget. You could have a bad reaction."

Alcohol? I was fourteen! Who did she think I was? Of course, I knew kids my age drank. I just wasn't one of them. Not that I told her that. Not that I told her anything. I just wanted all of this to stop, to go back to sleep for a long, long time. I put down the half-eaten sandwich and half-drunk juice and reclined on the hard mattress. If I never woke up again that would be awesome. I don't know when I fell asleep, but I did.

It was the doctor who roused me next. "Hello there. How's your throat?"

I sat up. "How did you know—"

"You were throwing up a lot. It's normal when you overdose on medication. Any other pain or discomfort?"

I shook my head, starting to notice my body, which felt really relaxed. I wasn't nervous or worried. It was as though my feelings were put away in a box for now. When I lifted my hand, though, it was heavy. The doctor noticed.

"Let's talk about your medication. We treated you for the overdose, to make sure there's no damage. So far, you are okay. I also put you on two drugs you will have to take for a while, a few months at least. One of them helps you to relax. It might make you sleepy. Don't worry," he assured me, "this is going to be all right. The medication will start helping you to feel better. Meanwhile, we need to figure out what's behind your depression."

It was the first time I'd heard the word applied to me. *Depression.* Was that the monster that crushed me every night?

"Can I ask you some questions about how you've been feeling?" He went through a questionnaire: Do you sleep too much? Do you have trouble falling asleep? Do you cry a lot for no reason? Do you ever feel worthless?

Yes, yes, yes, yes.

Do you ever feel like hurting yourself?

Yes.

Do you feel that you would be better off dead?

Yes.

It was the first time I admitted it aloud to an adult. Yes, I wanted to kill myself. I felt I had nothing to live for. I felt I was a burden to everyone around me. Yes, I felt I would be better off dead.

We chatted for a long time. I was surprised he didn't judge me. He didn't tell me I needed Jesus. He didn't tell me there was something wrong with me, something I needed to fix. He asked questions and he listened. He told me I was probably experiencing a major depressive episode, and that the churning feeling in my guts was anxiety. He told me I had to start sharing my feelings with other people, and that I had to remember depression and anxiety tell lies to my brain. He explained the medication. One was an antidepressant, and one was an antianxietal. One would help me feel happier, and the other would help me stop worrying so much. I might have to take them for months, maybe years, he said. Wonderful. More expense for my mom.

The doctor wasn't a fan of phones. "All that sharing and friending and liking isn't healthy," he said. "It's designed to make people feel bad about themselves. I can't make you do it, but if you can, stay off social media for a while."

No problemo. The last thing I wanted to do was communicate with anyone anyway. I could picture exactly how a conversation would go: *WYD?* they'd ask. *What am I doing? Oh, I'm in hospital because I tried to kill myself.* Awkward conversation, much? I deleted everything. Almost everything. For the next week, I kept checking my phone, so sure that it was vibrating under my pillow with scared messages from Ki-ki. I couldn't talk to her either, but knew she'd understand.

I was there for a week. Banana Kid never stopped trying to make conversation. I never engaged. Honestly, he was annoying AF. The larger reason I ignored him, though, was that I was sorting out how I felt after surviving my suicide attempt. I still had moments when I hated myself as strongly as ever. In those moments I was ashamed I couldn't even get suicide right. But every day I woke up feeling slightly better. I was cautiously glad I wasn't dead. I looked forward to talking to the doctor every morning, although when he passed on rounds, he always had his young flock behind him. He gave them pop quizzes on diagnosing and treating depression and anxiety in teens, using me as the case study. I was a guinea pig. I liked the doctor but I did not like having my private business used as a teaching tool.

The day before the doctor discharged me, he came to my room while my mom was there. After some pleasantries, he said, "Mummy, your daughter's struggling. She doesn't like school. She said she's not good at it. She feels like she doesn't fit in, and like she has no friends. Do you think that's a true reflection of her experience?"

Cynthia said nothing. She was an expert in the silent treatment. I had learned from a master.

He tried another direction. "How are things at home? How is your relationship?"

My mother's face was a closed door. "Fine," she said tersely.

"Any arguing? Disruptive behavior? Does she stop talking for days? Harm herself at home?"

Cynthia shook her head, no. She would never admit to a stranger that she had raised anything less than a perfectly behaved teenager. "I never saw anything out of the ordinary," she lied, brushing all my problems under a rug and slamming the door to the room shut. Her voice was so cold you could have crushed it to make a snow cone. I could see how much she disapproved of me. I wanted to curl up and disappear. Her disappointment was clear to me behind those frozen eyes. In spite of my new medication I felt a hot, hard mass start to burn in my stomach.

The doctor told her to supervise me at home for a few weeks, if possible. How? I wondered. She has a job. Would she have to take more time off to stay with me? "I am making arrangements," she told him coldly.

He handed her a letter in an envelope. "This is a referral to a counselor. It's important for her to start therapy as soon as possible."

I was on a plane to Canada two weeks later.

CHAPTER
FOUR

I cried all night after the Tacos and Tequila Incident. Then I stopped crying for a while but I wouldn't eat anything. And then I ate some crackers but I wouldn't talk. It felt as though I didn't sleep at all. I wallowed in my self-loathing and my terror of the world outside of my bed. There was nothing I could do but feel pitiful and hate everything about myself—and hate myself even more for feeling the way I did. Every few hours I heard that bubbling, babbling ringtone—it was Akilah, but I just couldn't face answering it. Just the thought of talking to anybody made me cry again even harder.

Jillian and Julie begged me to go with them to see Dr. Khan at his office but I couldn't imagine leaving my bed, let alone the house. At the end of the second day, Jillian brought the mountain to Muhammad, walking him to my room and leaving us alone together.

Dr. Khan's round, friendly face usually made me smile, but not today. I was sad, deep down in a dark hole where nobody could follow.

"Hello," he said softly when he entered the bedroom. "Jillian tells me you're not doing well. What's happening?"

I turned my back to him and stared at the wall. It had worked at the hospital and . . . Yes! Score! It worked again. Eventually, he left and told my aunt he'd come back another day. I had a feeling I could no longer convince him I'd be fine with just my meds, as I had when I'd seen him last month at his office. I sensed that a therapist was in my future.

I heard Dr. Khan give Aunt Jillian some sleeping pills (for me, not for her, though I can't imagine she was getting much rest, between my caterwauling and the sheer worry she must have felt) and tell her to keep an eye on me. Since I'd already proven that I was capable of taking an overdose, Jillian kept track of my meds and doled them out to me as prescribed. The new sleeping pills knocked me out for hours at a time. From what I remember, I didn't think about anything much in between bouts of sleep. I mostly lay around feeling wretched, feeling a sharp, inner agony that I couldn't touch or see but which was nonetheless like a gaping wound somewhere inside of me. I did want to die; that I remember. Death was the only thing I felt would stop the pain of my existence. Like turning out a light. Snap. Done.

Akilah called again when I was awake one time. I picked up.

"Oh my God, I've been so worried! Are you okay?" Akilah's

panic showed on her face and in her voice. She was frantic. "You didn't go and do anything to hurt yourself—?"

I groaned an apology to her. Tears trembled in my eyes. "I'm alive. But I can't talk, okay? I'm sorry." And I hung up on my very best and only friend. Which made me feel so bad I started to panic again. What was wrong with me? Why couldn't I just be normal?

Tears, snat, anguish. Lather, rinse, repeat.

Julie and Jillian took turns sitting with me practically around the clock. I would fall asleep with my head in Julie's lap and wake up in Jillian's arms, hardly knowing one hour from another. I had never felt so wretched.

When Dr. Khan returned, I grumbled that house calls cost a fortune, and he said he didn't usually make house calls at all. "I know what it's like to be a new immigrant. It can be really scary. Everything's big and strange. And it all moves so fast." He added, "I don't make this exception for everybody, though. Jillian and I go way back. You're important to her and I want to help her support you. She didn't want you to go back to a hospital so soon after your recent stay."

First: Immigrant? *Whaaaat?* But I brushed that aside. I'd obsess about it later, I was sure. For now there were other details to unpick. Until he'd mentioned it, I hadn't even thought about a house call as a big deal. And hospital? It never crossed my addled mind once. Then it hit me like a full-on *Cobra Kai* roundhouse kick how terrified Jillian and Julie must have been that I would have tried to kill myself again. It was true, though, I had had a Classic Nervous Breakdown. Again. This time I actually felt relieved I hadn't died, as much as I had wanted to be dead when the dreaded canyon yawned in my belly. I was alive and I was . . . happy to be alive? Maybe not quite happy to be alive, but at least sort of happy I wasn't dead. It was a lot to process. I wouldn't let Jillian leave, gripping her hand like I did in the bathroom during the Tacos and Tequila Incident. *Stay, please,* I begged with my eyes. She smiled and squeezed my fingers to let me know she understood, and that she would stay. Julie leaned against the doorframe, looking elegant despite the fretful look on her face.

"What do you think led to this panic attack?" Dr. Khan asked baldly. He'd been so careful when we last met. I realized he'd decided to try another tactic.

"Was it . . . because of the boy?" Julie nervously prompted.

This whole episode wasn't really anything to do with Josh or his dad. Yes, it was the awfully uncomfortable dinner that proved to be the tipping point, but honestly, it could have been anything pushing me over the edge. That afternoon, I should have known that something was up. I knew I was feeling sadder and more hopeless and scared than I had been since coming to Edmonton, and the awkward dinner somehow, in my tangled reasoning, seemed to be all my fault.

Dr. Khan smiled at me hopefully, waiting for me to say some of those things out loud. At first, I couldn't. Though I had been under Dr. Khan's care since I had been in Edmonton, he had never seen me crash. In our first long appointment he asked me stuff I recognized from sessions I'd had with the doctor in Trinidad. Usually Dr. Khan didn't push me. He talked more than I did, because I didn't say much in our sessions. This time he asked a lot of questions. Like, a lot. And he refused to let me avoid them.

I kept glancing over at Jillian and Julie. My mother had responded very coldly to this part of everything when I was in hospital, making me feel as though my whole existence was inadequate and that I was only making things harder for her as a single mom. But Jillian and Julie didn't react like that. They looked worried while the doctor asked the first few questions—not worried I'd say something to embarrass them, but worried that I was so unwell. It was all new to me. I wanted to see how they would react to my answers. Dr. Khan finally asked me, "Do you want them to stay or are you going to work with me today, really work?"

I sighed. It was scary. But if the alternative was that disgusting hell of the last couple of days, then . . . "Okay. They can leave. Thanks, Aunties."

They both said *you're welcome* at the same time. They grinned a little and ducked out of the room to give us some privacy, holding each other's hands on the way.

"Tell me what's been going on," Dr. Khan said. He was not as formal as my first psychiatrist at the hospital in Trinidad, and talked to me like I figured a big brother would, if I had one. "Are you taking the meds I prescribed?"

I nodded. I finally talked, in a low, shaky voice. "I do everything you said to do, Doctor. I take the medicine. I exercise. I try not to worry about things I can't control. But I don't know. Sometimes I just feel . . . You ever spin around really fast with a water balloon and then let it go? I feel like that."

"Like the person spinning?"

"No. Like the balloon. I'm so scared. And when I get scared I get mad. And then I get sad because I'm so scared and mad and I can't do anything about any of it. It makes me . . ." I slumped forward, dropping my chin to my chest, and wrapped my arms around my middle to hold back some of the pain that threatened to surge.

"Oh." He sighed. "Antidepressants don't work overnight," Dr. Khan said, telling me what I already knew. "They take weeks to be absorbed into your system." In my case, he explained, the medication I had been on since my troubles began took about three weeks to take effect, and as long as two months to really work. "You feel the meds have been helping? Do you feel better or worse now than when you came to Edmonton?"

"Kind of better? They help me not feel so sad. Sometimes." Sometimes I still felt like I had the Grand Canyon in my belly, but to be honest those times had been getting further and further apart until the Classic Nervous Breakdown.

"Your going out, walking, swimming, and going to the gym also help," he said. "Jillian told me all about your busy days."

I had no idea they knew or cared what I did every day. I told them about my activities, but neither of them made a big deal out of it. They just let me be. "I read that it's good for you to try to do stuff when you're depressed."

"Yup," Dr. Khan said. "Depression and its close buddy anxiety are mental illnesses, but they have physical aspects as well. Most people don't realize how much exercise can help."

After I left the hospital, I'd done a lot of Googling of depression and anxiety. I learned that plenty of teens and even some little kids suffered with depression, even though adults might question what they could be depressed about. I knew that part of the cause of my problem was my brain chemistry. People who have depression don't make enough of this brain chemical called serotonin, which scientists think helps make you happy. The most popular kind of antidepressant helps your brain build up more serotonin so you feel happier. But your brain also makes serotonin (and other feel-good chemicals) when you exercise and avoid stress, when you're hugged, and from sunshine. I can't honestly say if I had been feeling better because of the medication or because I was out of my horrible school and away from my judgy mother. I was walking and swimming in that weak-ass Canadian sunshine, and getting plenty of hugs from Jillian and Julie. And still, for the past few days the paralyzing pain and self-hatred had come back as strong as ever.

For as long as I could remember, my anxiety kept me up at night. I would worry about failing at school, every stupid thing I had ever said, global warming, my mother, the father I never knew. Fear would steal my dreams, gnawing at my guts and closing up my throat. Akilah told me that I worried for nothing, but her words meant little to me and certainly didn't help me sleep when I was staring up at the ceiling in the middle of the night. When they first gave me the medication for my anxiety it made me doze, which was great for my sleeplessness. As the weeks went on, though, it was less and less effective. This meant my nightly vigil over all the bad things, real or imagined, had started up again about two weeks before the Tacos and Tequila Incident.

"Kiddo, you worry too much," Dr. Khan said. "Really. Remind yourself that worrying won't change anything. Do what you can do, and the rest is out of your hands, and that's okay."

"I'm so dumb," I muttered.

"And please," he begged, looking me straight in the eye, "remember what I told you about being gentle with yourself. Give yourself a break. You're a good, valuable person. And you're not dumb."

Dr. Khan and I talked for about twenty-five minutes, with him doing most of the talking. He wrapped up when Jillian came back to the doorway trying not to look concerned.

"We're done for today, but are you writing in your journal?"

I nodded.

"But you know," he said to me in a gentle voice, "you have to see a therapist. I don't usually do this type of talk therapy, I told you."

"But—" I tried to resist, but both he and Jillian gave me such stern looks that my protestations crumbled. I guessed I would have to consider talk therapy with someone else after all. Soon, I promised them. Yeah, right.

He talked to Julie and Jillian in the corridor outside my room for another few minutes about what to expect. I could hear him. "She'll be very quiet, probably, and might take some time to get back on her feet. Don't push her to do too much, but don't baby her either. She's sick but not physically helpless. Try to coax her out of bed and even out of the house. She should not be on her own for a little while, until the suicidal thoughts subside. Encourage her to exercise. Once someone's with her, she should be fine. And make that appointment ASAP."

"I'm on it," Julie chirped. "Booked an appointment in three weeks. . . ."

My stomach heaved. I'd have to do that stupid questionnaire with another doctor? Dig up all that crap about my mom? Tell yet another person what a waste of space I felt I was? Yuck, yuck, yuck.

"What about having people over? We were going to have a barbecue next weekend," Jillian said. "We were going to cancel it."

"Nah," Dr. Khan said. My heart dropped. I'd have to see people? Why, oh why? "She has to find ways to cope with her condition within a family. If she finds it gets to be too much, she can retreat to her room. Don't force her. Encourage her to remember that other people can be fun to be around. You might want to tell your friends to give her a lot of space. Just say she's a moody teenager; they'll give her a wide berth."

Jillian walked him to the front door. Julie came to me and sat on my bed, holding my hand. I was able to have a conversation for the first time in days. Talking to Dr. Khan had helped, in the end. But I felt so embarrassed about the way I had cried, the way I had felt, and the trouble I'd caused over the past few days.

"I'm really sorry about this," I muttered to her.

"Oh, muffin," she said. "Don't worry about it. We knew this might happen. We're here to support you. Whatever you need."

"Yeah. But it's so . . ." I didn't know what to say. I felt ashamed of how I had behaved, even though I knew that I really didn't have any choice about it. Clinical depression and anxiety disorders have minds of their own.

"Hey. Don't worry about it," repeated Julie with a firmness I seldom heard in her sweetly musical voice. "What do you want for dinner?"

I shrugged. While talking to Dr. Khan had helped, making decisions still felt like one of the hardest things.

"Curry?"

"Uh. Yeah," I said. Julie's chicken curry was amazing. And she made it with basmati rice and about six different side vegetables, each served in a little silver bowl. My favorite was dal, warm yellow split peas made into a puree. All that cooking should have taken hours and hours, but Julie somehow did it in two. Jillian returned and Julie slipped out to start dinner. In moments I smelled the wonderful aromas of frying garlic and geera, or to Canadian Aunty Julie, cumin.

Jillian was looking at me with a little half-smile.

"Chickie! You had us really scared for a while."

"Yeah, I'm sorry," I repeated. "I'm too much trouble."

"Nonsense! We love you. And we knew you were dealing with this when we invited you to stay here," she said, echoing what Julie had said. I think they had worked out a spiel in advance.

"Want to go outside?"

I shook my head. I had no idea what day it was or what time it was but I knew that it had been quite some time since my last bath. I felt sticky and dirty and could feel a layer of grit on my teeth. I smelled like old, wet dog. "Think I'll take a shower."

She smiled encouragingly, helped me up, and led me to the bathroom. She sat on the edge of the bathtub while I reached into the medicine cabinet for toothpaste. The floss and mouthwash looked lonely on the now barren shelves. There wasn't a single razor or bottle of pills in sight. I felt a little contempt for myself. What kind of person puts their family through this? Why shouldn't they hate me? I am useless. But then I saw Jillian's dark eyes looking back at mine in the mirror. There was no hate in them. There was only love. She seemed glad to sit there and keep me company.

I brushed my teeth. My aunt moved to lean on the sink while I had a shower. My back hurt from lying in bed so long. I washed my hair and body slowly, with shaking hands. I dried off with the towel Jillian held out for me.

In my room I pulled on some clean clothes and sat on the edge of my bed for a while next to Jillian, both of us silent. By then the house was full of the pungent smell of curry and the aromatic scent of basmati rice.

I suddenly realized that my last meal had been the barely eaten chicken at Tacos and Tequila. Remembering that reminded me that I had had my freak-out session in the presence of the Cute Boy, the best-looking boy I had ever seen in my entire life, who miraculously seemed to be interested in me! I groaned and hid my face in a pillow. Jillian put her hand on my shoulder and rubbed it lightly, no doubt gearing up to deal with another meltdown.

"Don't worry," I said, my voice muffled by the pillow. "I'm

not going to trip off. I was just remembering how I messed up in front of—"

I gulped my last words down. "What?" Jillian asked.

"Nothing," I lied, and then got up and we went outside to the deck. The tubs of summer flowers in the backyard seemed way too bright after my seeing nothing but blank walls and bed linen for days. There was a light breeze blowing. The flowers bobbed their heads in the rustic-looking planters. A few leaves blew off the neighbor's maple tree, falling on the neat, green lawn. I picked up a rake and went to gather the stray leaves. When I'd pulled them into a little pile, Jillian and I sat on the patio chairs and just watched the dancing flowers. My hands were still shaking.

After a while, Julie joined us. "Dinner's almost done," she said, wiping her hands on a paper towel. Dropping an absentminded kiss on the top of Jillian's head, she took a seat next to us. "What do you want to do tomorrow?" she asked me.

"Dunno," I said.

"Swimming or gym?" Jillian said, mindful of the doctor's words about exercise.

"Gym, I guess," I said after a minute, thinking of my comfy new sneakers.

"We should take turns taking her around," Julie suggested to Jillian. "I'll take her tomorrow, you could do the next day."

"Don't you think I should take her out first?" Jillian responded.

"Um, hello?" I said. "I am sitting right here." Julie looked abashed, but only a little bit. "Besides, it doesn't matter. I'll be okay with either one of you." People fighting over me wasn't something I was accustomed to, but I could get used to it.

Julie beamed at me. I didn't say it out loud, but what I meant was that she was equally as important to me as Jillian—who looked at me with a big grin when she caught on.

"Well, look at us," Jillian said. "One big happy."

Maybe not happy, not yet. But one big something, for sure.

CHAPTER
FIVE

Jillian and I were in the kitchen when the phone rang. Since hardly anybody ever called other than Cynthia, we knew what that *ring-ring* sound probably meant.

"Hello, yeah?" I said when I picked up.

"'Hello, yeah?' Is that how you answer the phone?" Her voice was sharp. My mother was irritated at my lack of whatever, blah, blah, blah. As usual. *You suck, kid. I wish you were a better daughter.*

"Sorry," I grumbled. "Hello, Mom. How are you?"

"Fine. Still trying to catch up on work. You know those people, always putting paperwork on my desk in a complete state and I have to do everything. . . ."

I zoned out. When she called my name for the third time I came back to myself with a snap. "Yes, Mummy?"

"Let me talk to your aunt. You clearly have nothing useful to say."

My face burned. Without a word more I handed the phone

over to Jillian. My aunt watched me with a frown. I couldn't tell if she was pissed at me or her sister. Probably me.

A little voice in my head chimed in with Dr. Khan's reminder to say nice things about myself. Okay, okay. Maybe Jillian was annoyed at her sister, not at me.

"Cynthia! How are you?!"

Jillian was always nice on the phone with my mom. They were sisters, after all. They had been close once, really close, before Jillian left Trinidad.

"Oh, things are going well. . . ." She told Mom about her new contract, leaving out the LGBTQ connection. My family was full of things better left unsaid.

"Oh, she's doing great." She threw me a look. "Cynthia, I don't want you to panic, but she had a little setback.

"Small. But yes, a breakdown.

"Four days.

"No, she didn't go to the hospital.

"But—

"Yes, she saw a doctor.

"Cynthia, lis—

"Cynthia! Listen to me. She's okay. No, you don't need to come. She's doing much better now. It was last week and the doctor has seen her. She's doing fine now," she repeated.

At that point I drifted back to my room. I had heard all I wanted to hear. Obviously my mother was going to try to convince Aunty Jillian to send me back to Trinidad. I hoped Jillian would stand up to her.

Minutes or hours could have gone by as I thought of how I'd

have to leave Edmonton and everyone and everything in it. I was lying on my back, staring up at the plain white ceiling, when my aunt came in.

"Well, that was hard," she announced. I didn't reply. "Hey, sport." She held my chin and turned my head to look at her.

"Am I going back?" It was all I wanted to know.

She looked surprised. "No! I told her you were fine, didn't you hear me?"

I snorted. "As if she listens to anybody."

"She listens to me. I'm her big sister, you know! I told her you were in good hands. Am I right or am I right?"

Reluctantly I smiled. "You're right."

"Scooch over," she said, lying on the bed next to me and taking my icy hand.

"Cold hands, warm heart," she intoned, a relic from her childhood that I, too, knew from my own. In a lot of ways, things hadn't changed in the Caribbean since she was a girl. "Baby, you're going to stay here until you're ready to go home. Don't worry about your mom, okay? I'll handle her."

Little tears started slipping from the corners of my eyes. "I never want to go back home."

"You will, one day. But right now you can just stay here until you feel ready. Don't worry. You'll be my little girl until then. And this can be your home."

I buried my head in her shoulder and cried.

After a while my sobbing stopped. I wiped my face with the back of my hand and just lay there smelling her spicy, warm perfume. I sniffed. "What's that you're wearing?"

"Patchouli. It's an herbal perfume. Very hippie-dippy," she said, winking and grinning.

"Are you a hippie?"

The grin stretched farther. "Nah, just a good environmentalist. Nobody does animal testing for patchouli," she explained. "Like any good lesbian I have to believe in a cause."

The way she said it was funny but I could tell she was partly serious.

"What does that mean?"

"Well, I was joking," she said, resting her cheek on my head. "It's a thing people say about gay people. That we identify with causes—animal rights, the environment, homeless people, immigrant rights, the poor." She thought about it for a second. "I guess, because we know what it's like to be in the minority and the underclass. We know what it's like to have no voice so we try to speak for others who don't either."

I digested that for a while. "What's it like?"

"Patchouli?" she asked, pretending to be serious. "Okay, okay," she giggled as I pinched her arm. "What do you want to know?"

"Well . . . what's it like being . . . you know. Gay."

"I don't know what it's like being anything else, so that's a really hard question for me to answer. It's just normal for me. What's it like being straight?"

I shrugged. "I dunno. Normal, I guess."

"See what I mean? But I do feel sometimes—not so much anymore, but I used to feel like I wished I were like you and like Cynthia. I do want babies and a 'normal' life. So it's kind of weird not having those things, but I couldn't really imagine myself any other way."

"Did you ever have a boyfriend?"

"Yup. Did you forget I told you Nathan and I dated? Way before I knew I was gay. We stayed friends, though. And Josh is my godchild, as you know. I wish I saw more of him. Sweet kid. Josh, I mean, not Nate. Nate's a pain in the—"

We laughed at the same time. I was glad she shared my opinion of Nathan. He was arrogant and self-centered and I didn't like him one bit.

"Was he always like that?"

"A jerk?"

I nodded.

"Uh-huh. He grew up very privileged and I suppose he never had to think about other people. He likes 'exotics' because they give him a glimpse into the other side but—" She shook her head. "Why am I having this conversation with a fourteen-year-old?"

" 'Cause I asked?"

We laughed again.

"Are you an 'exotic'?" I asked.

"Yup. So are you, to people like him. You'll meet lots of people here who think that you're some kind of collector's item just because you have a Caribbean accent and dark skin."

I already had. I thought about the young policeman who tried to talk to me at the bus stop, and others I had met at the library and the gym. "White people are always surprised that I speak English and wear normal clothes and stuff," I said. Then I thought about Julie's version of "normal," the clothes she called "Desi high fashion," and reconsidered my language. "Western clothes, I mean."

"Right. Not everybody's like that but some people are. Nathan married a Jamaican, that's Josh's mom, and I think Nate was always surprised that she was brighter and better educated than he was."

I chuckled.

"But Josh seems like a good kid," she repeated. She looked slyly at me. "What do you think about him?"

I blushed and bit my bottom lip. If the earth had opened up right at that moment it would have been awesome.

"Ooh! Looks like somebody has a crush!"

"Aunty!"

"Oh, all right. I'll stop teasing. I have to give you fair warning, though: I'm inviting them over to the barbecue."

"Not the barbecue!" I said in dismay. Maybe it wasn't too late for them to change their minds. Alas, they were following the doctor's advice and taking life back to its ordinary level. I didn't have to participate, my aunt told me, but I'd be expected to come out of my room and say hello at least once. Hesitantly, I agreed. "But don't tease me about the boy, okay? It makes me feel bad."

"Agreed," she said. No teasing, but I had to get ready to talk to the most gorgeous boy I had ever seen, in my temporary home. This time, I hoped I could do it without having a complete collapse.

I called Akilah as soon as Jillian closed the door.

"Ki-ki!" I wailed.

"What? Are you okay?" She had obviously prepared herself for the worst. It had been ages since I had talked to her. She looked scared, her eyes open wide and her mouth trembling. "I was so worried!"

After apologizing for ghosting her, I calmed her down and

told her about the awful past week, the sleeping pills that knocked me out, Dr. Khan and his advice to exercise and his threat—um, I mean promise—that I would seriously start talk therapy soon.

"Why are you hating on therapy so much?" Akilah asked.

I was scared of what the therapist would say when I told her or him about my deepest secrets. When normal people hear that you want to kill yourself, they treat you like you're crazy. But when you're crushed under that monster and you can't breathe for the pain, nothing makes more sense than wanting to die and make the pain stop. Talking about it was almost as scary as feeling the feeling itself. "I just don't want to. Julie's already made the appointment," I wailed. I was being dramatic, but it was a front for real fear.

She sat at her kitchen table. Her mom was cutting up vegetables in the background; I heard the rapid whack of a blade on a chopping board and could imagine the kitchen redolent with pungent *chadon beni,* the dark green leafy weed we use for seasoning food in Trinidad. A wave of homesickness hit me. There were so many things I wanted to say but didn't want Aunty Patsy hearing. And top of the list was the gorgeous kid, Josh. Gesticulating to Akilah that she should leave the kitchen had no effect. I typed in the message bar, *GO TO YR ROOM!!! WE HAVE TO TALK!!!!*

journal session 4

I think about color a lot. Even more now that I live in Ed-monton, since the color of my skin marks me as different from most of the city's population. When I was walking down the street, I would be one of a handful of black faces in a sea of white; there's more salt than pepper here, if you know what I mean.

Home home, brown skin is the norm. Most of the people who live in my country have either African or Indian ancestors. Walk through downtown San Fernando, my hometown, and you'll see a spectrum of complexions ranging from palest ochre to darkest ebony. It's beautiful to me. As a child I took it for granted; my world was full of brown people, people who looked like me. They lived next door, loaned me books at the library, drove the buses I rode, read the news on TV, and ran my government. I hardly ever saw white people in real life. On TV sitcoms, yeah, all the time. But not doing ordinary stuff like taking out the garbage. Here, white people were my neighbors, my librarians, my bus drivers, the news anchors, the city council, even the garbage men.

Being black in a black country doesn't mean race isn't important, though. I grew up accustomed to people referring to me by the color of my skin: I was a dark-skinned girl. Not just me, either; so-and-so was a red-skinned lady; so-and-so was a brown-skinned fellah. I had a neighbor everyone called Blacks because his skin was so dark. Nobody said it out loud but skin color mattered. The lighter your skin, the more desirable you were for a job, for anything really. A light-skinned mixed-race girlfriend with long, wavy hair was the gold standard if you were a boy, no matter your race. Girls freaked out over light-skinned boys—"red man"—as though they were some kind of prize. Even Ki-ki said her grandmother wanted her to marry someone who would "add some milk to the coffee" and give her light-skinned grandchildren one day.

As a bony, dark-skinned girl with short, kinky hair, I felt I was nobody's first pick. Matchstick. Charcoal. Bun-bun. Those were some of the nicknames the other kids called me. My personal fave was Corbeau, after the pitch-black vultures that lived on garbage and dead dogs in the dump. In my primary-school graduation class photo I was a dark, unsmiling smudge with huge eyes, hiding in the back row behind the lighter, smiling faces.

When I told Akilah the Cute Boy was light-skinned, she screamed. "You? I can't believe you have a crush on a red man!" I rolled my eyes at that. I didn't like him because he was light. He was super cute. Like super. Cute. And taller than me (how rare was that?!). Besides, I had never had a crush on anybody at all, red man or not. When I told her Josh's skin color, describing it

93

as caramel brown, she laughed at me. "He making you not only thirsty, but hungry, too! Caramel?" I knew she was only teasing but I seriously thought about what she said. Why not say caramel? I'm the color of dark cocoa. She was the color of milk chocolate. It wasn't my fault all the good colors for brown happened to be named after food. Besides, I've read stories where white people were called "olive" or "peaches and cream." Those are food, too, right?

Josh was smart and cute and so cool. He was a catch; there could be teenage girls all over Brooklyn swooning for him. Though Ki-ki always told me I was pretty, I never believed her. If a dark, skinny girl with picky hair was pretty, why weren't there more people like me at home home in the advertisements on TV? Pale Indian faces adorned billboards for skin lightening cream, Bollywood movies, and rum. Light-skinned mixed-race people sold pretty much everything else, from car batteries to rum. (Everybody sold rum.) I have to admit they put a lot of dark-skinned soca singers on billboards. I liked Fay-Ann best of all. She had short hair, even shorter than mine!

My hair was another thing. It was never long to begin with, and the tightness of its curl made it seem even shorter. Every time she combed it, Cynthia wished out loud that I would straighten it like she did hers, and save her the ordeal of putting her hands through the thick coils. Every couple of months she herself went to the beauty salon and paid a lot of money for her hairdresser to put a chemical paste into her hair to take the kink out of it. The cream smelled like old pee and burned her scalp, leaving painful sores that scabbed over the next day, but when she walked out of the salon she had straight hair that swished past her shoulders, for a while, at least. When I turned twelve she asked me if I wanted to do the same to mine. I said no. She couldn't understand why. The first week of the third term of school, right after Easter, I took a pair of paper scissors from my pencil case and cut my hair off. I don't know why. I ketch a vaps, like we say home home. School had been agony that day; maybe that was it. At lunchtime I could barely stop myself from running into traffic if only I could make a dash past the security guards at the gate. At home, finally alone and away from all the noise of my school, I looked into the mirror and saw my picky hair. It was all I could see. Not my clear skin or my big black eyes or my full lips or my high cheekbones. I saw only the hair my mother hated. It filled me with frustration. I didn't pause before I started to snip. Mom was blue with rage when she saw me standing in my bedroom with that little heap of black plaits at my feet. She marched me straight to the barbershop to get my hair evened out, because of course it was an awful cut, patchy and rough. I got a long lecture about making the best of my looks, and that included what little hair I had left. A woman's hair was her glory, she said again and again. When it grew out enough, she said, I would get a weave. I sat in that barbershop chair, hearing the buzz of electric clippers and feeling the sting of the alcohol the barber sprayed on the back of my neck when he was done, thinking I would never want to stick someone else's hair into my own. Why should I? There was nothing wrong with my own hair, was there? And if there was something wrong with my hair, was there also something wrong with me?

CHAPTER
SIX

The morning of the barbecue was crisp and clear. Julie was up early, mixing meat, mushrooms, and onions into a slurry that, she assured me, would turn into the most delicious hamburgers I'd ever tasted. Jillian was out buying charcoal and paper cups and I was assigned to rake the lawn, clean the bathrooms, and put out fresh towels. I also had to change the sheets on the pullout sofa bed, in case anyone stayed over afterward.

It was about ten in the morning when I finished my chores and gave a thought to the fact that I had absolutely nothing to wear. Yeah, I had T-shirts, jeans, shirts. But nothing in my wardrobe was an outfit I considered worthy of the occasion. It had to be something really special.

"Uh, Julie?" I said weakly.

"Sugar? What's up?" She was, by this time, vacuuming the living room. She switched off the vacuum cleaner and looked at me expectantly.

"I have . . . I have nothing to wear."

Jillian chose that moment to walk in. She screeched. I wasn't sure whether she was horrified that she was related to me, or thrilled that I was finally showing interest in something except the color and texture of the ceiling paint.

"That's wonderful!" Julie yelled.

Jillian dropped her bags by the kitchen door and hurried out to the living room. "Oh, baby!" I was engulfed in a spicy patchouli hug. "Let's go immediately. We can pick up some things at the mall in a hurry." She turned to Julie. "You have—"

Julie waved us off with a huge grin. "Go before the child changes her mind."

Jillian and I got into the car and sped to the mall in record time. I didn't have a chance to stress out before she practically dragged me into a store called Sweet Harts, which had half-naked mannequins all over showing legs and boobs and bellies and butts to an alarming degree. I never would have expected her to choose this store, and not these clothes, given the way she dressed herself. Then I remembered seeing pictures of her the way she used to look in her teens, before she left Trinidad. She was pretty and girlish and prone to frills. A lot of pink eye-shadow too.

"Uh, Aunty," I called out.

She didn't hear me. She had a tube top in one hand and a miniskirt in the other and was sizing me up with a glance that made me feel a little afraid.

"Aunty! I don't think this is my speed," I said more firmly.

Her face fell. I was wearing a plain black T-shirt, black joggers, and Birkenstocks. While I wasn't ready to meet the most gorgeous boy in the world looking like that, I sure wasn't going to see him with my so-called boobs and tiny butt hanging out.

"Of course, baby," she said, ruefully putting the clothes back on their hangers and turning for the exit.

Outside of the shop, I spotted another store. Regular jeans and shirts were on the mannequins in this window.

"What if we try this one?" I said.

We walked around in there and still there wasn't anything I liked. Nothing screamed *This Is What to Wear in Case You Lime with the Most Gorgeous Boy in the World.*

We tried a third store and finally hit the jackpot. It was a soft lilac dress; Aunt Jillian said it had cap sleeves and an empire waist-line, falling in an A-line skirt just below my knees. It wasn't too girly-girl but it wasn't severe, either. Against my dark skin it looked divine. The Birkenstocks didn't look so hot with it, though. And the socks definitely had to go.

"We need to get you some sandals. I mean nice sandals," she said, grimacing at the ones I had on. They were comfy and practical but not exactly cute.

I got some white sandals with low heels. They fit okay, though not as comfortably as the clunky Birkenstocks. But these sandals were adorable. They made my toes look long and elegant, I noted with pride and some awe. Jillian was so excited about the whole ensemble I didn't have the heart to tell her I planned to wear the dress over a pair of skinny jeans. On the way out we passed a kiosk with cosmetics. I lagged behind, throwing meaningful glances at the makeup, and Jillian gave in with mock exasperation. A tube of lip gloss later, we were out in the car and speeding back home so we could keep preparing.

People started coming over at about two in the afternoon. Jillian fired up the big grill on the deck in the warm sunshine and Julie laid out some chips and salads while the meat sizzled. By four o'clock the place was full. A blur of faces passed me by. I stuck to the living room, playing DJ with Jillian's old iPad and an aux cord connecting it to the stereo system. I was reading the track list on a Prince greatest hits collection when I heard a husky voice say hello.

I jumped about a foot.

Josh was wearing a white T-shirt and black skinny jeans strategically ripped at the knees. He had on a bandanna, too, tied like a headband. And a thick gold chain. Really? He looked like a young thug. I was a little disappointed. The boys I knew at home who dressed like that usually had nothing to say except dumb things they picked up off of hip-hop and dancehall music, stuff they didn't really understand the meaning of but mindlessly repeated after they heard it in some song. And they had really limited tastes. His next words, therefore, came as a complete surprise to me.

"Oh, snap! Is that a greatest hits? See if it has 'I Wanna Be Your Lover' on it. Oh, man. That is the baddest love song ever. RIP to the Artist."

"RIP," I murmured back. I was thinking that I didn't know if I agreed with him on that song's position as the greatest love song ever. In fact, I think I definitely disagreed with him. But who would have thought that he would know the works of my favorite singer? Not me. I was thrilled.

Okay, maybe Prince wasn't my very favorite singer. But he was up there with the top ones.

"You like Prince?"

"Oh, yeah. No doubt. He was the best musician of his time, bar none," he said, stooping to my level, literally if not metaphorically. Taking the tablet from me, he read off the titles on the album's track list. "You gotta run this track!" he said, pointing to 'When Doves Cry' on the list. "I have loved this since I was a kid watching that old movie with my mom. We do it every year."

Hmm. You never know about people from just looking at them.

I must have looked at him funny because he suddenly got self-conscious. "What? It's my moms, yo," he muttered.

"Uh. Nothing."

"Okay. Hey, nice to see you by the way."

Zing! Pow! Pop! That was my heart exploding, if you didn't get it. I mumbled something in response, too busy blushing to be able to actually speak. For once, I wasn't completely freaked out by the possibility that I was saying or doing the wrong thing. I had a huge smile on my face. My heart was bucking like a rodeo bull but gradually it calmed itself. As we played the music, the funky falsetto took away my nervousness. Track followed track and we were perfectly chill with letting them play on shuffle. In about twenty minutes we said maybe five words to each other, but it was a friendly kind of silence. I was about as relaxed as ever when my aunt came in with Nathan.

"You kids having fun? Can we get something other than Prince now?"

"One more song," Josh and I said at the very same time, breaking into laughter as we said it.

"One more!" Nathan sighed. "There must be something else you guys can agree on."

"How about this?" Josh, who had been riffling through her music library, highlighted Santana's *Supernatural*. I raised one eyebrow and nodded approvingly. He had good taste in music as far as I was concerned. But I wasn't entirely convinced; could be he was making the best of a bad situation and didn't really like this stuff. It was just that the most recent dancehall Jillian had in her library was some Super Cat circa 1990, and as for hip-hop, *The Miseducation of Lauryn Hill* was the most up-to-date of the lot. Her tastes ranged to the old and romantic, rather than the young and urban. She had a lot of folk and jazz music, some calypso, and, of course, Bob Marley, which was practically a prerequisite for any music collection. But the stuff that I listened to at home—Rihanna, Beyoncé, Drake, Popcaan, Kendrick Lamar, Machel Montano, Bunji Garlin—was conspicuously absent from Jillian's iPad.

I seemed to be wrong in my judgment of Josh's tastes. He continued to pull stuff out that gave further lie to his gangsta uniform. The Beatles; Simon & Garfunkel; Earth, Wind & Fire; and Parliament-Funkadelic joined Santana in a growing playlist. His sparkling gray-green eyes squinted in concentration as he checked more music out. I got to my feet and stretched. "Hey, want some sweetdrink?" I asked.

"Huh?"

"Soda. Pop. Want some?"

"Yeah, sure. Coke, if you have it. What did you call it?"

"Sweetdrink. It's what my mom always calls it. It's a Trini thing. You wouldn't understand."

"Sure I would," he scoffed. "Unnu nah recognize me a fi 'alf Jamaican, mon?" It was a pretty bad accent but he seemed proud of it. If his mom lived in the States, it wasn't a stretch to consider that he'd probably never seen Jamaica.

"Riiiight," I said. "Let me get that Coke."

Julie was in the kitchen, wearing an apron that said "Kiss the cook," so I did.

"You're in a good mood," she observed as I poured two glasses of soda.

Santana's old duet with Rob Thomas, "Smooth," came on. "Uh-huh, I sure am! We're playing back-in-times music," I said as I did a little three-step.

Julie grimaced in fake agony. "Is this considered 'back in times' already? God, I'm old. How are the burgers?" There was a tall stack of them next to her. Red meat wasn't a big mover that afternoon; all the bean patties and other vegan stuff were gone already. I grinned in response, licking my lips hungrily at the perfectly cooked meat nestled in fresh, soft buns. I gathered up a paper plate of three along with the drinks. It was a precarious arrangement. As soon as Josh saw me carrying the wobbling freight, he sprang to his feet and took the plate and a glass from me.

"Hope you eat beef," I told him over his thanks. I settled next to him on the couch and bit into my sandwich. Burger juice spurted out and spattered on my lap, right on my new dress. "Oh, man!" I whined. Now I'd have to change it. And of course, I had nothing else to wear.

"Oh, come on, it's just a little spot," he said, whipping off his bandanna and dabbing at the stain. It was cute. I was blushing so hard I was nearly glowing. He unfolded the bandanna and draped it on my lap like a napkin. "So you don't mess up your nice outfit anymore," he added.

He thought my outfit was nice? Yay!

We listened to more music, talking little, and ate some chips and salsa. By nine o'clock his dad came around again, a glass of wine in hand. Nathan was pretty drunk, by the sound of it. He slurred his words a lot and took much longer than usual to finish his sentences.

"Looks like I'm spending the night here," Josh said. "Hope your couch is comfortable."

The way he said it made me feel he had been in this position before, but I didn't want to ask. I didn't have to, as it turned out.

"He's drunk a lot these days. He's breaking up with his girl-friend." He shook his head. "Man, you must be so glad your aunts are in a stable relationship."

I nodded, rendered mute for the moment. Hearing the words coming from his mouth made me feel a bit surreal. These aren't things we talk about at home home. I thought that, at home, Jillian and Julie would have probably passed as just close friends or roommates. And no matter how drunk somebody's dad was, they never would have said a word about it.

"It sucks that my dad is in this up-and-down thing. I never know if she's going to be at the apartment when I get home or not. Some vacation."

"I'm sorry. That sounds like it sucks."

"Yeah," Josh agreed, "it kind of sucks. I only get to see him once a year and he doesn't realize that he's wasting our two months together by being drunk all the time."

"Your dad has been drunk every day since you've been here?" I asked, incredulous. That sounded a bit intense.

"Well," he considered, "maybe not every day. But often. At least he doesn't get violent or anything, just . . . so boring. I have to hear about every girlfriend he ever had when he gets into it," he said with a little laugh, shaking his head. "Your aunt was the one that got away." He paused, passing his hands idly through his curly hair and momentarily distracting me from our very serious conversation. "How do you like living with your aunts, anyway? Julie told us the other night that you might be moving here permanently."

My heart skipped a beat. I might be moving here permanently? That was news to me. But there had been Dr. Khan's "immigrant" comment. I shoved the thought aside for the moment. It was too distracting. Instead I focused on answering his question. "I don't know. I like it a lot, I guess. But I'm not in school, and it's not like real life yet, you know? I don't have any friends here."

I paused. Mentally I added that I didn't have any friends at home either. I just had nothing in common with most of the kids I knew. That started me worrying that I was weird, and that Josh would never want to hang out with me under normal circumstances, say if we weren't the only teenagers trapped together at my aunts' barbecue. Akilah was the only one I could talk to without feeling like a complete extraterrestrial.

As if she had heard her name called in my mind half a world away, the bubbling ringtone began.

"What is that noise?" Josh asked. "Wait, is that Skype? My dad uses that!"

I grabbed the phone, excused myself, and took the call in the bathroom.

The first thing I did when I answered was to shriek silently. Akilah saw me freaking out and was immediately worried. "What? What? What?"

"Relax," I said. "It's just that I'm. With. The. Cute. Boy."

"What!!!"

"Oh my God, you have to meet him. Ki-ki! Help me! I don't know what to say! I'm so dumb and awkward. What if he—"

Akilah interrupted my rant right there. "Come on, remember you're supposed to say positive things about yourself. You're not dumb. Awkward, yes. But that's where I come in. Let's go meet your man," she teased. I shot her a look, but took the phone back to the living room and introduced Akilah to Josh, turning the screen so he could see her and she could see him.

"Hey, nice to meet you," he said in that very velvety voice. "Could you please explain why you don't just WhatsApp like regular people?"

"She turned off all her social apps," Akilah said without any further explanation. "She only has Skype." When I turned the phone back to myself Akilah's expression showed that she was very impressed with Josh, very impressed indeed. She gave me two thumbs up. I made a monkey face like a child, sticking out my tongue and waggling it enthusiastically.

"What?" Josh asked, grinning but obviously puzzled. I guess monkey face is not a good look for me. Darn it.

"Babes, it's really loud over there," Akilah complained, shifting attention from my doctor-recommended-social-media-hermit situation.

"Can we go to your room or something?" Josh suggested.

Decamping, we left the adults to the mercy of Jillian's iTunes. I led the way to my little bedroom. It was perfectly tidy and I was glad I hadn't left the contents of my closet out on the bed after my earlier flap about what to wear. We sat on the floor, backs against the bed. I held the phone up so both Josh and I could see Akilah.

"So," she said, breaking the silence, "how did you guys meet?"

Josh told her the story. He left out the part about how I got sick in the middle of dinner. She already knew about it, though. "I'm glad my dad is friends with your aunts," he concluded, chuckling.

Which reminded me. "I really need to talk about my situation with Julie and Jillian. They are great, but I'm still not used to them as a couple," I confessed to Josh and Akilah.

"Country bookie to the bone!" Akilah said.

"Like a country bumpkin," I jumped in and translated for Josh because, from the look on his face, he was clearly confused by the Trinidadian expression.

"Josh," Akilah continued, "to be honest, where we come from you never see a gay couple. And if you do, you'll never see them show PDA. There are places where that will earn you and your lover a beatdown."

"True?" he murmured. "I hear things like that about Jamaica but we never go there."

"For reals. Can I tell you something?" I asked. He glanced up at me with those stunning eyes. I melted a little inside but then steeled myself to continue to talk about my living situation. "It's great. They're great. But I just don't know how to feel about them being . . . well, you know."

He raised an eyebrow and lifted his palms in puzzlement.

I sighed. "You know. Gay." I said it low, spat it out like a bad word.

Akilah cackled on her end of the phone call. "You can say the word, chile! I know you can! Say it loud, say it proud!"

We all laughed, and then Josh said, "You can say 'gay.' Kids I know say 'queer' sometimes. It doesn't change who people are, if they're gay or straight. I mean, yeah it does, but a good person is a good person. You know what I mean? Folks are just folks."

"That's easy for you to say. Where I'm from, you just don't call people that word unless it's a joke or an insult. Nobody's out as gay. I can't think of one single gay couple at home, not even like a celebrity couple. I don't know. People just hide it. For me this is . . ." With my hands I mimed my head exploding. We all laughed again.

"It's not important, trust me." He looked over at me meaningfully. "Can I tell you something?"

I nodded.

"My mom has had a boyfriend but when I was little she had a girlfriend. Some of the times she seemed the happiest were with her girlfriend, I think. Being gay or bi or whatever doesn't change who she is or how she treats me. That's the important thing: your aunts love you, don't they? And they show it." He looked frustrated, and fiddled with his own phone as he talked. "I just wish my dad was more . . . caring. Sounds dumb, coming from a guy, right?"

"Are you gay?" Akilah joked lamely.

He glared. "That's not funny."

"Yeah, I know. Sorry." She looked abashed. He grinned and waved it away. I liked him even more.

CHAPTER
SEVEN

Josh and Nathan weren't the only ones staying overnight. A couple of other people did too. Most of the adults stayed up late into the night, taking over the living room, drinking wine or coffee and watching movies. Some ended up sleeping on the carpet, and some on the sofa.

We talked to Akilah for hours. Josh had music on his phone and I had a Bluetooth speaker so we listened to songs on that. It was mostly hip-hop and dancehall, but there was some rock music in there too. Akilah ratted me out, telling him that I was an old fan of Justin Bieber and he said he understood and liked me anyway. My heart sang.

"What about your school?" Akilah asked him.

"What about it? It's normal. You know."

"Well, actually, I don't. Remember I live in Trinidad. School here is much different from what I see on American TV."

He laughed out loud. "School everywhere is different from what you see on American TV. Nobody looks that good."

I refrained from pointing out that he looked like a super-cute extra on *The Vampire Diaries.*

He continued, "I'm going to be a senior at Audre Lorde Charter School."

"Where's that?" Akilah was asking all the questions I wanted to ask but was too shy to speak out loud.

"Oh, in New York."

"Duh," she said. We cracked up again.

"Brooklyn, to be specific. Close to where my mom and I live. It's okay, I guess. I'm doing a bunch of pre-pre-law stuff, like about the constitution and society, for extra credit. I'm applying to Columbia and I want to go to law school there eventually. . . . But I don't know if I'm going to transfer and spend my senior year up here with my dad before college." He turned those hazel eyes on me. "What about you?"

"I'm in third form, which is like"—I did some quick math in my head—"about ninth grade?"

"You're that young?" he said, surprised. "Thought you were about sixteen."

I ducked my head. "Nah. Fifteen in two months. I'm kind of tall for my age."

"You can say that again! How tall are you?"

"A little under six foot," I said.

"With that height and your looks, how come you're not a model? If you lived in New York you would have been spotted by now."

"I know, right?" Akilah yelled. "She's so pretty and she doesn't even know it."

"Oh, please," I said.

"No, seriously. You're really pretty," Josh repeated Akilah's assurances.

I turned away, scoffing, "Blah, blah, blah." A boy had never called me pretty before. Tall, skinny, dark girls with short hair didn't get called pretty at my school. Mostly they got called "black and ugly."

Josh was baffled. "Tell me you're kidding," he said. I said nothing.

Akilah sucked her teeth. "I've been telling her that forever but she never believes me."

"Okay, but don't say I didn't tell her so." He let it drop and turned back to me. "Tell me about your school."

"Well," I said, "I do boring stuff. English, Spanish, social studies, integrated science, geography. It's coed. The boys do electrical stuff and woodwork and the girls do sewing and cooking. We could do it vice versa but nobody really encourages you to do that, so we stick with tradition. It's not considered a good school but it's okay. I mean, it's kind of rough."

"Kind of?" Akilah jumped in. "With some guys selling weed behind the technical block, and some girls getting into fights . . . they stab each other over boyfriends and stuff."

"Fights . . . like with knives?" he asked.

"Yeah. It's rough. But it could be worse: they could have guns," Akilah said, deadpan.

"It's okay, it's not that bad," I said, desperate to stop talking about it.

"Wow. Why don't your parents transfer you to a different school?"

"Parent," I corrected. "My mom's a single parent. Never had a dad." He nodded but didn't say anything, waiting for me to continue. "And with school, well, it's not that easy to move kids around from school to school," I said. "There's this assessment exam you have to do to get into a high school and I failed."

"You didn't fail!" Akilah squawked.

"Okay, true, I didn't fail. I just didn't do well enough to go to a great school. My mom thinks I should live with the consequences of my actions." I did a good imitation of my mother's serious voice as I put bunny ears around the words she had so often said. *Bitter much, kiddo?* I asked myself.

"So she'd rather you went to a school you didn't like, where there are drug dealers and violent gangs, so you could live with the consequence of your actions? Sounds crazy," he said.

When he said it like that, I had to agree with him. But I had to stick up for my mom. "She means well."

"Besides," said Akilah, "those schools are where the majority of kids end up in our country. It's normal."

"Uh-huh." He didn't sound convinced.

"It's not that serious," I said, trying to be casual. "Can we talk about what you heard from your dad? That I might be here permanently?"

Akilah gasped. "Oh no! You have to come home!"

"Yuck," I said, gagging dramatically. "I hate that place."

"No, you don't," she rejoined.

"What is there to like?" I said. "Oh yeah, I can't wait to get back to my tropical paradise. All we ever hear about is how many murders and kidnappings we have every year."

"Really?" Josh was shocked.

"Yeah," Akilah reluctantly agreed. "Crime is terrible. As a girl nobody wants you out at night by yourself. They say you could get kidnapped, sold into the sex trade."

"For real?" His widened eyes were joined by a gaping mouth.

"Or how about the truly loveable public utilities?" I grumbled. "We get power outages . . . how often, Ki-ki?"

"Once a month, maybe," she allowed.

"Wow. When the lights go out in New York it makes the news," Josh said.

"And let's not talk about water."

"What do you mean, water?" Josh asked.

Akilah fielded that one. "You know how you open the tap and water comes out when you pay your bill? Well, where we come from, most of the country doesn't get water when it opens its taps. Not every day, anyway. It's rationed."

"Tuesdays and Saturdays," I added. "That's when we get water. All the rest of the week we have to use water from our tanks."

"And what if your tanks are empty?" Josh asked.

"Salt," Akilah said.

" 'Salt'?"

"Yeah. Salt. Nothing, zip, zilch, nada," Akilah said. "You can use the toilet at the mall."

He shuddered. "It isn't that bad; you're exaggerating."

"I wish," Akilah replied. "It can be really awful here, compared to some places. But it's beautiful, too," she chided me. "Come on, admit it!"

"Well," I said, "the hills are kind of spectacular. And the people are great. Sometimes."

"When they're not trying to beat up gay people?" Josh asked sardonically. "Your country sounds lovely. I can't imagine why you'd ever leave."

"But it's home, you know?" Akilah said. "Your home isn't perfect either. I mean New York is the most dangerous city in the world!"

"No it isn't," I muttered.

"Whatever," she said with a sigh of exasperation. "My point is that whatever is wrong with it, it's my home. I won't leave. This is where I belong."

I thought about that for a second. Was it where I belonged?

Josh changed the topic. "My mom sounds like the opposite of your mom. She's really overprotective of me. I had to go to the best school—it's public but a charter school, which is like a private public school. . . . It's hard to explain," he ended, looking at my befuddled expression. "Whatever. It's a good school, no knives—or guns. But like I said, I really want to spend some time with my dad before I start college."

"Have you ever lived with him before?" I asked.

"Yeah, when I was a baby, I guess," Josh said, picking at imaginary lint on his jeans. "But I don't remember much about that. I mostly know him from spending summers in Canada. I see him every year. It's hard because I live in the States and he lives all the way up here. This place is like *the boonies,* man. And it's sooooo white!"

"For reals!" I chimed in. For a few minutes he and I traded tales about Trinidad and Brooklyn. At home we'd be just faces in the crowd—in Josh's case a gorgeous face in the crowd. We of the brown skin stuck out in Edmonton.

"It's nice to get a break from my mom, too." He bit his lip, hesitating, before he spoke again. "She's depressed and it's like, every day is a drama just getting her to eat breakfast and take a shower. Sometimes." He quickly added, as if he didn't want to be disloyal to her even in her absence, "I love her a lot, you know? But it's kind of tough to be around her twenty-four-seven."

I turned it over in my mind for all of two seconds before I jumped to his mom's defense—a woman I'd never met. "I'm sure she's trying her best. Depression isn't easy to cope with."

"Yeah, it's tough. But she makes it harder. She doesn't go to her therapist, she drinks too much sometimes, she skips taking her meds other times. She's a great mom but I just wish she'd realize that all that stuff—the medication, the therapy, yoga—is actually good for her, and not just something we're forcing her to do because we hate her."

In San Fernando, Akilah's mother yelled at her for being on the phone too long. She made her apologies and promised to Skype me again the next day before signing off.

Josh and I continued to talk about his mom. "So what's she taking?" I asked. "Some of the medication can have awful side effects, you know. It can make you fat, sleepy, dopey."

"Uh-huh, I know," he muttered, looking at me strangely.

"She's on Prozac. She says it messes with her sex drive. How come you know so much about this?"

"How come you think?" I asked darkly.

"Oh snap! You too?"

I nodded, without looking at him. I didn't want to see the look on his face. I didn't want to see him judging me.

"Hey," he said, awkwardly but gently, "it's cool. I mean . . . it's cool."

I snuck a glance at him. "For reals?"

"Yeah," he said, a small smile on his sweet lips.

Not only was he cute and smart, but he had great taste in music and he was understanding, too.

"At least you think so. People at home would never understand. If it ever came out in school that I had attempted suicide, that I was clinically depressed and living with a chronic mental illness, I would be persecuted relentlessly," I confided. "Where I come from a lot of people think mental illness is either demon possession or deliberate bad behavior."

"Are you serious?"

"Yeah," I said. "My own mom . . . she thinks I'm just being overdramatic."

My mother's attitude was, sadly, typical. I could count on one finger the number of people who would be understanding and sympathetic to someone with a mental illness. And did Akilah really count in this equation? She was a kid like me. She couldn't protect me.

"You really tried to kill yourself, though? How come? What happened?"

I told him the short, ugly story, ending with my brief hospitalization before Cynthia passed me over to her sister. "When it's bad, I really hate myself," I said. "I don't know why. I just want to die. Like I shouldn't be alive. Like I don't deserve it."

He looked at the door, not at me, shaking his head. "Word. I feel you. You sound like my mom. It's not true, though. You do deserve to live." His hazel eyes turned to me. I felt like I was in a sniper's crosshairs. "If you ask me, I'm pretty glad you're alive."

If he was the shooter, I was happy to be hunted. Game. Over.

We talked a bit more, listening to some of his music too. He was deeply into trap, the strange, hectic hip-hop music from the southern US. I knew some trap songs, the ones that had made it to the radio at home. "Oh, I like this one: 'Baking soda! I got baking soda!'" I sang along. But I wasn't really a fan. He played his favorites and explained what the songs were about—many were about selling drugs.

"I don't get it," I finally admitted.

"Word," he said, grinning. "You don't have to. We can like different things and still be cool." I fiddled with my fingers. He took one of my hands in his. "Are you nervous?"

My heart was in my throat. Josh's hands were warm, soft, strong. Next to his light brown skin mine seemed extra dark. I didn't know what to do. Should I sit there with my hand limp? Should I touch him with my other hand? What should I do?

Akilah and I had strategized about this on our last call. She had raised the possibility that he might try to kiss me. I had wanted to dismiss it completely but she had insisted. If someone likes you, no matter where they are from, she said, they're going to try to kiss you if you two are alone. Her advice was to "be natural." Since I'd never kissed a boy (or a girl, for that matter), I had no idea what "natural" looked like in this context. My heartbeat raced like tassa drumming.

Weakly I tried to pull my hand from Joshua's grasp but he held on, stood up, and gave me a tug, pulling me over to sit on the bed as he did the same. We faced each other with our legs folded like yogis, his sneakers taken off long ago and parked by the bedroom door, and my sandals tossed beside them. Those hazel eyes pinning me down. He leaned toward me and I could smell his cologne, fresh and breezy, and his breath, minty from the gum we had chewed after finishing our burgers. I closed my eyes.

His lips barely, delicately touched mine.

And then the door swung open. "Oops!" Nathan chortled, more amused than apologetic for barging in on us at this key moment. "Sorry to interrupt! Josh, I just wanted to let you know we are definitely staying the night."

Hastily pulling away from each other, Josh and I dropped our hands into our laps and looked at Nathan innocently.

"Sure, Dad," Joshua mumbled.

"Hey, no funny stuff, okay?" Nathan teased his son, stepping into the room and ruffling his curls. "I know she's beautiful, but you have to let her get to know you first, son," he teased. I could tell he was drunk, but under the slurred words and cloud of alcohol fumes I could also tell there was a spark of parental concern. "These island girls will break your heart." Nathan theatrically winked at me before stumbling out of the room again. Gross.

Our moment was over. The music played on. I stayed seated

on the bed and he slid back to the floor. We faced one another. Before long, both of us lay down, head to foot, he on the carpet, me with one arm trailing off the side of the bed fiddling with the comforter. It was chill. There were no words between us as we listened to songs. Physically, we were farther apart than before . . . but by the time I fell asleep we were holding hands.

I woke up the next morning with a crusty feeling in my mouth and a great big smile on my face. Josh's curly hair was just visible under a drift of blankets on the floor next to my bed. Through the open door I heard the blessed sound of silence. I was evidently the first up.

Or maybe not. I heard the sound of water running in the kitchen and bet myself that Julie was cleaning the mess left over from the party.

Climbing over Josh's inert body, I crept out to get a glass of juice from the fridge. As I suspected, Julie was scrubbing away at the counters, getting rid of a vicious maroon stain next to the sink.

"Bloody red wine," she muttered as I walked in. "Hey, muffin. How was your little party?" she asked with a tiny smirk.

I blushed. "Oh, it wasn't like that," I started to explain.

She laughed, swatting me with a damp tea towel. "I should hope not! I was kidding, honey. I'm glad you're making a friend. I was worried that you'd never talk to anybody outside this family ever again." Her teasing smile was gentle. I felt happy and excited and couldn't wait to tell her about the whole thing.

"We just played music. Talked. He's really nice," I said. I

wanted to explain more, about how easy he was to talk to, how he understood about my depression. How we sort of kissed. Almost. But the words were caught up in my chest and wouldn't come out. Instead, I mumbled again, "He's really nice."

Her smile told me she understood.

I poured some juice and drank it, feeling my stomach beginning to rumble with hunger. I glanced at the clock on the microwave and was surprised to see it was after eight already.

"If I were back home I would have been in church by now, starting Mass," I told Julie. "Mom insists we go to church every week, and I don't even know why. It's not as though she's all that devout."

"Maybe she likes the routine of it?" Julie asked. "The predictability? Could be nostalgia, too. Every time I go to a *puja* I feel like I'm a little girl, safely back at my *aji's* house in Toronto. We cling to rituals, don't we? Humans are funny."

I could kind of understand some of what she said; I liked familiar routines, too. But I didn't see the point of going to church if you didn't want to be a real Christian and were doing it only for form's sake. Or for memories. My memories of church were one long blur of boredom and skepticism. A God might exist. Did he need to be worshipped and adored or was that our shtick? It seemed like a waste of time—but maybe that was just me. I shrugged.

I was still standing in front of the fridge. I opened the door and stared, trying to figure out what was quick and easy for me to have for breakfast.

"Here," said Julie, reaching around me to grab a stack of cheese slices from the dairy compartment and a bag of English muffins from a packed shelf. "I'll toast one for you."

"Thanks. Julie, can I ask you something about Jillian?" I was finally ready to ask about that conversation I'd overheard, when Jillian said she wished she was my mom instead of Cynthia.

She responded with a cautious nod. "But really if you have something you want to know you should ask Jillian herself. She won't bite," she teased.

I opened my mouth to ask the question and flaked. I shoved the muffin there instead. I wasn't ready for this conversation.

I ate the crisp, warm bread with melted cheese, mulling over what she had said when Josh's dad came in, wearing a T-shirt and boxers. He was stretching and yawning and scratching, looking like a man from a movie, obviously hungover. If I wasn't sure before, I was convinced then that I didn't like him much. How such a boor could have made such a considerate son was beyond me.

"Morning, ladies," he said, in between huge yawns that smelled of sour liquor. "Julie, what has your niece done with my son?"

I said good morning and looked intently at the fridge and shoved more into my mouth so I wouldn't have to say anything else. While they talked I took the opportunity to go use the bathroom, washing my face and brushing my teeth and generally trying to look slightly less jacked up than I had when I crawled out of bed.

I needn't have worried. Josh was still fast asleep when I tiptoed back into the bedroom. In fact, he slept until nearly noon. His dad woke him right before they were to drive back home. He only had time to give me a quick hug, squeezing my hand and promising, "I'll Skype you," before leaving with his dad. I thought I'd probably see him again soon. I hoped I would, anyway.

When Akilah called that evening, we did an exhaustive analysis of the whole three-way conversation, and then further discussed every second of the almost-kiss and the hand-holding that followed it. We agreed we'd have to wait until the next time I saw Josh to make further judgments. But she thought it was a great sign he was going to install Skype on his phone just to message me. I still hadn't turned any of my social media accounts back on. It took him another day, but eventually I heard from him: *Sup. Miss u.* Immediately, I formed a group chat with him and Akilah.

That week drifted by with me staying mostly at home listening to music, watching movies from Jillian's enormous collection, and surfing the net. I toyed with the idea of starting a new Instagram account, but then changed my mind. I wasn't ready yet to do anything so public. The idea of anybody crawling through my pictures and making comments filled me with terror. Instead I contented myself with obsessively watching BuzzFeed videos on YouTube. Josh and I messaged each other briefly every night. Nothing serious, just about movies we'd watched and music we'd listened to that day. Slowly we were getting to know each other. Emphasis on "slowly." But I held on to the memory of the way we had almost kissed, and the tingly feeling of my skin on his when we held hands.

I was at peace, starting to feel like the world wasn't such a bad place. I saw Dr. Khan and I was starting to get the hang of writing in my therapy journal.

Then my mom called again. From the airport in Toronto. She was coming to Edmonton. She was almost here.

journal session 5
_____

Dr. Khan keeps pestering me to talk more about my mother.

What else is there to say? I don't know. Dr. Khan said to just start writing about her in my journal and see where it takes me, so here I go.

Cynthia gave birth to me fourteen years ago. She was sixteen; she finished her O-Levels with a baby bump. I have a picture of her when she was fifteen, and one of her with me at my christening, but there's nothing from when she was pregnant. I don't know my father. There aren't any pictures of him either. I don't know how they met, or even who he was. My birth certificate is blank under "Father's Name."

That doesn't bother me as much as Ki-ki thinks it should. Everybody has a dad, she says. Yeah, of course. Men and women have sex and that's how you make babies. Duh. Yet women get pregnant and men don't know about it unless the women tell them. Cynthia never told me what happened. Sometimes I imagine that they were childhood sweethearts and he died young. Who knows? Cynthia sure wasn't talking. She never got married. As far as I knew, she didn't have boyfriends, either. Sometimes she went on dates with other singles from church, but nothing ever came of it. Cynthia wasn't exactly warm and welcoming.

Still, my earliest memory of her is nice. I think I'm looking up at her from my crib. It's night and she's smiling at me. Maybe it was a dream.

I grew up with her. We lived in my grandparents' house. It wasn't a terrible place. My grandfather was a bookkeeper who lived long enough to know his unwed teenage daughter had disappointed him by getting pregnant. My grandmother, a housewife, followed him to the grave when I was six. My memory of Granny Rose is blurry. She was sick for a long time, since I was a baby. I hardly remember her, except that she was bedridden and her room was always dark and smelly. Going to kiss her goodnight was like entering a haunted house. She would stare at me. It was terrifying. But in old pictures, she was proud and stern and pretty. Her hair was a long, shiny plait flowing from below her church hat right down to her breast. She looked nothing like my mother. We got our looks from my grandfather's side of the family.

I remember Granny Rose's funeral better than I do her. There were a lot of flowers. Like, a lot. Plenty of old people smelling of camphor and rum, singing hymns I didn't know. Plenty of strangers on the church steps kissing me and telling me how much I looked like my late grandpa. I remember piling into a big car to go to the cemetery with my mother, some cousins I didn't know, and Aunty Jillian. To be honest, I mostly remember Aunty Jillian. She was so different from my mother, so happy and smiley, even though it was a funeral and everybody was kind of sad. But I could tell they were sisters. They talked the same way. And when Aunty Jillian wanted to, she could make my knees shake with one harsh word just like my mom could. With Granny Rose dead, they were all the family I had left. Cynthia didn't make any effort to keep in touch with her other relatives. She depended on no one but herself.

Cynthia always worked. I spent a lot of time at the library, where she left me as long as she could from the time I was old enough to read. She grumbled that her job was boring and that the school that employed her took her for granted, but she had to do it anyway. "Everybody has to work to live," she always said. "Nobody owes you anything." Over and over, she said that I had to be responsible for myself. "You can't rely on anybody else. People will disappoint you." That was how she was, and that's what she expected of me. We didn't talk much at all, not like mothers and daughters in the movies. We didn't have warm, loving conversations over tea and biscuits.

I've never seen my mother cry. She's just not the crying type; she'd quicker hit you than let you see her weak or wounded. I think part of what she never accepted about my illness was that it seemed like weakness to her. Mom expected everyone to be able to just deal. Lonely? Deal with it. Man left you pregnant at sixteen? Deal with it. Hate your job? Deal with it. Don't break down, don't trip. Just quietly and efficiently deal with whatever it is that's bothering you. Deal with it alone and shut up. When I got my period for the first time, she handed me a pack of tampons and sent me to the bathroom. I read the instructions and figured it out, eventually. While Akilah was celebrating getting into the convent school, I resigned myself to my fate. The school I'd passed for was infamous: understaffed and with a reputation for student violence. But I had sat the exam. I had to live with the consequences of my actions.

I don't blame my mother for my illness. I don't blame her for sending me away, either. I'm glad she sent me to Canada. I'd tried my mom's method and I'd still wanted to die. Everybody isn't wired the same way. Jillian and Julie are the best thing to happen to me. They let me be myself here.

CHAPTER
EIGHT

Though I wanted to go into hiding and never come out, Jillian and Julie made me go with them to meet my mom.

The airport was a cavernous, frightening place, like a cross between a market and a supermall. It had a huge, high ceiling, with ranks of uncomfortable-looking plastic chairs. Nothing was familiar, even though I had only recently come through there myself. Everywhere I looked, I saw miserable passengers who seemed like they were lost dragging enormous suitcases around. They congregated below the arrivals and departures screens, watching the lines of information continuously updating. In between, there were uniformed flight crews pulling smart black carry-on cases on wheels, striding purposefully from one end of the airport to the next. Though it was daytime, neon lights lit the book, candy, and souvenir stores. A stuffed horse made of fluffy, plush fabric called my name, but I didn't stop to say hello, just threw it a longing look before trailing after Jillian and Julie to the crowded arrivals hall where we would greet Mom.

After checking a screen to confirm her flight had arrived, we squeezed into a spot between a family of four redheads and a Jamaican couple. I kept looking around for something I could recall from my own arrival.

"Blurry memory" does not cover it. Try "Good night, Port of Spain; good morning, Toronto! Good afternoon, Toronto; good evening, Edmonton!" Probably for the best. I cried myself to sleep the first few nights at my aunts'. Who knows what that flight would have been like without the medication to knock me out.

My Edmonton airport memories were vague, but wasn't there a baggage carousel that snaked out of a hole in the wall, carrying suitcases and bags? Wasn't there a sound it made? *Clang-bump-hummmmmm.* Maybe. "Remembering your trip here, muffin?" Julie asked.

Impulsively I said, "Nah. I was thinking about the baggage carousel. Can I ride on it?"

"No!" Julie chuckled. "Please don't try it. It's dangerous and I'd have to tackle you. I'm too old to be scrambling around on the airport floor. So undignified."

We laughed together. It was easy to be myself around her. I was comfortable. So comfortable that I had blurted out loud one of the many random things that crossed my mind from time to time. Fortunately, I didn't have to worry that I'd disappoint her by saying something ridiculous. It still felt hard to be completely honest. However, I tried. It was mortifying to admit it, even to Julie, but there was a hole in my brain and I couldn't remember arriving in Edmonton. "I don't remember this airport, Julie. I took a lot of tranquilizers so I wouldn't freak out on the flight. I was not exactly in good shape when I traveled, right?"

She stopped laughing. "True," she agreed. "How are you doing? All set to see your mom?"

I didn't get a second to answer. My mom must have parachuted off the plane before it landed. There she was, the first Toronto arrival, dragging a case behind her.

"Cynthia!" yelled Jillian, pleased as punch to see her sister. Jillian's last trip home had been ages ago and they hadn't seen each other since. My trip into exile had been planned over Facebook and phone calls. We traveled to Port of Spain to the Canadian High Commission for an interview that was so quick it passed like a dream. I was out of the hospital one day and in the air soon afterward, heavily medicated and flying as an unaccompanied minor to my recovery in Edmonton. I'd had a passport as a form of identification since I was small, but this was the first time I'd gone anywhere with it. The single immigration stamp on my passport was smudged. The maple leaves on its edges as blurry as my memory of arrival.

Mom was looking really pert and pretty in jeans and a crisp white shirt. I guess having no child to look after suited her to the bone. It was all right by me, since being away from her suited me just fine too.

Her hug was stiff. Our initial conversation was just how I had pictured it would be:

"How are you?"

"Fine. You?"

"Fine."

"How is everything at home?"

"Fine."

It took all of thirty seconds, probably, to run out of things to say to her. Yes, I was taking my medication. No, I wasn't feeling ill. Yes, the doctor said I was improving. I loved it here. No, I didn't miss home. At all, I lied.

I guess she was a bit perturbed that I would come right out and admit that I was happier in Canada than at home, but she didn't say anything. I supposed I was in for it later on, though. To my surprise I felt some anxiety when I saw her, but nothing like the rushing-to-my-doom overwhelming despair that would normally have accompanied such a meeting just a couple of months ago. In fact, I could honestly say that I really felt . . . fine. I hoped it would last.

She had just the one suitcase, which Julie quickly grabbed and hauled off to the car. We took Mom to lunch at a steakhouse and she and Jillian made conversation about everything at home. Mom kept staring at Julie, and I wanted to kick her for making Julie seem like some kind of freak, but Julie handled it like a pro, neither ignoring Mom nor pointedly staring back. I felt a bit bad at first, but as the evening progressed I got more and more infuriated.

It had been about two months since I had seen my mother. Time had changed us both.

She and Jillian were laughing over some old schoolteacher they had had when I interrupted without preamble.

"I don't want to go back."

Julie immediately tried to play it off. "Hey, muffin, we can talk about that later. . . ."

Mom wasn't having that, though. She engaged immediately.

"It's time for you to get back to your real life. You have to go back to school. Your place is at home."

"My real life is in a place where nobody wants me around, nobody understands me, and nobody really cares if I live or die?" I asked, the light of challenge sparking in my dark eyes.

My mother was outraged. "What nonsense! What self-indulgent nonsense! You go on as though you had no friends."

"I have no friends!" I shouted.

"Don't be ridiculous. What about that girl Anika? Akua? The one you went to primary school with."

My jaw dropped. She couldn't remember my only friend's name! "You don't care about me at all."

"Of course I care about you! I might not always understand you, granted, but I always do my best by you, child. How dare you come with this attitude, these accusations!"

Jillian tried to calm the turbulent waters. "Cynthia, you know she's just exaggerating. Of course we all know you care about her and whether she lives or dies. She's not being literal. I think she means that she doesn't feel accepted for who she is."

My mother's mouth was a thin, unsmiling line. "Who she is, is my daughter. Her place is at home, with me. Whether I understand or accept her or not."

The waiter came with the bill and Jillian tersely handed him a credit card before turning back to her little sister. "I really think it's bigger than that, Cynthia. You have to understand that she's ill. Without love and acceptance she'll be worse off—"

Mom snorted. "Ill?" Clearly, despite all the doctor had told her after my pill-popping incident, she wasn't convinced I was actually sick. As far as she was concerned, depression was some kind of self-induced and entirely frivolous condition. In other words, I was probably making all this up. Or rather, I was making all this up to spite her.

Nothing was further from the truth. But I knew I couldn't convince Mom over steak and salad. I shut my mouth.

The ride back to the house was tense. Over the stiff silence, Jillian and Julie pointed out landmarks to Mom's stony face, and I *steups*ed under my breath a couple of times before Jillian told me to cut it out. Sucking your teeth to an adult was a no-no here, too, it seemed. Finally we were home. We pulled into our street just as a bus roared off in a cloud of hot air. *It's the Eighteen,* I thought automatically. *That's my bus!*

Mom got out of the car with a flounce, and walked around and stood by the trunk, tapping her foot impatiently. She was in a hurry to finish the discussion. So was I. Jillian wasn't, though. She eased the suitcase out of the trunk and up the steps to the front door, inviting Mom to come in. Julie and Jillian gave her a quick tour, ending at my bedroom. Although Jillian left Cynthia's suitcase in my room, my mom would sleep on the foldout living room couch during her visit—her choice. She could have slept with me in the guest room. Mom glanced around at the small room, painted a pale pink, with its white eyelet cotton curtains and comforter and white furniture. It was a girl's room; it occurred to me for the first time that Jillian and Julie had probably decorated it for me just before I got to Edmonton. I could see, from the tightness around her mouth, that the thought had occurred to my mother at the same time it did me.

I saw her eyes flicking over the neat room and knew she was mentally comparing it to my room at home, which was even smaller and was never this organized. I kept this room tidy because, even though Jillian was family, I wasn't really home home and didn't want her to feel put-upon by my presence any more than was necessary. Somehow I wanted to make the best possible impression, in spite of everything. I had to rely on myself. My mother, who knew me from before I was born, would have understood all that without me saying anything, and I saw something flicker in her eyes as she took in the room, the neatly stacked books on the night table, the absence of clothes strewn on the crisply made bed. Even the floor was clean, with no shoes thrown haphazardly around as they would have been back home. She looked at me, that same expression in her eyes, looked back at the room, and walked out without a word. She could have chosen to be proud of me for finally learning to pick up after myself. Instead, it seemed, she chose to be offended that my behaviors had changed here.

It was hours before bedtime and we had yet to talk about the purpose of her visit: to take me back.

She led the way to the deck while Julie went into the kitchen to get everyone some cold drinks. It was afternoon, warm and muggy by Canadian standards, which after two months had suddenly, it seemed, become my standards. I didn't know how I would cope if I went back home to the furnace-like heat and ponderously humid air. My hair, cut so short when I had come, had grown out a bit into a wiry Afro, sort of like Jillian's, but thicker. I took a hank of the tight strands and started twirling it between my fingers and thumb, making little curls that stuck out from my head at right angles. I could tell from Mom's disdainful look that she didn't appreciate the aesthetic, but it wasn't meant to be a fashion statement, just something to do with my hands.

"Have you been keeping up with your schoolwork?" she asked, checking out the pristine lawn and pretty flowers as she talked.

"Not really," I admitted. "I go to the library a lot, but mostly I read whatever I feel like. I am teaching myself French, though," I added.

"French?" Frowning, she turned back to me.

"You didn't tell me that," said Jillian with a surprised grin. "I could have helped. *J'adore le français,*" she said, with the requisite guttural pronunciations.

I saw my mom tighten her mouth, so I changed the subject. "I bought a dress," I said. "Want to see it?"

She looked wounded. Too late, I reflected that for years she had tried to get me to buy a dress of my own accord—with no success whatever. And now, here, I'd finally done it. Without her.

The afternoon wasn't going well.

Julie came out, as fresh as a breeze of summer flowers, carrying glasses of lemonade on a tray. She was such a caretaker, it was almost funny, a real Wilma Flintstone. Not that Jillian was flat-footed Fred to her Wilma, just that Julie was so concerned with keeping things running clean and smooth. I envied her easy way with both housekeeping and people. Remembering how she effortlessly handled Nathan in his caveman wake-up mode, I admired once again her ability to smooth people's feathers as she graciously handed my mom her glass of lemonade, doing a little dip at the knees to keep the tray steady.

"Oh, look at you with your bunny dip," Jillian teased her.

I was confused. Bunny? Seeing my confusion, Jillian explained. "Julie used to be a waitress in Toronto for a while at this gentleman's club—"

"Read: strip club," interjected Julie.

"—and they taught her how to do something called the 'bunny dip' so she could serve drinks without bending over and showing her cleavage," Jillian said.

"Yeah, showing cleavage was strictly reserved for the girls on the poles," Julie joked.

"The move was invented by the Playboy Bunnies, for their club," Jillian explained.

My mother was less and less amused as the moments ticked by. "You worked in a strip club?" She made it sound like Julie had made a living selling crack outside a kindergarten or something.

"It was only for a couple of months, when I was an undergrad," Julie said. I liked how she said it without tension, as if there was nothing to be ashamed about. As if it was just a job.

Mom's top lip was curling farther and farther into a sneer. "Doesn't sound like a great place for a woman to work," she said.

"Actually," Julie replied, "it wasn't bad at all. Management was very strict about customers not being able to touch the employees. And the tips were great," she threw in with a wink.

As fascinated as I was by the idea of strip clubs and bunny

dips, I was anxious to get to the meat of the discussion. So was my mother, apparently, as she cut to the chase first.

"Jillian, it's time for this child to come home with me."

There were tears in my eyes.

I couldn't help it. I was sad, angry, frustrated, but mostly horrified at the thought of going home. I just wasn't ready yet to face the same old places where nobody cared about me, the school where I didn't feel like I belonged. In any case, hardly anybody tried to actually teach us anything there; they had given up on us before we had even started. As a school clerk herself, my mother ought to have known that but she didn't seem to care much whether I did well or didn't; whether the school I went to was good, bad, or indifferent; whether the kids I sat next to in class were going to grow up to be pharmacists or drug dealers. If she cared, she did an awful lot not to show it. If she cared, she was awfully good at pretending otherwise.

It wasn't just the school. I didn't hate it all the time; it was okay some days. It wasn't anything specific that made me unhappy there. The teasing didn't happen all the time, and mostly the other kids left me alone. And it wasn't really my mother. It was the whole country—the smallness of it—that seemed to close in on me sometimes. I could understand why some people like Jillian couldn't really be comfortable living in a small place like that, where to be gay or lesbian or whatever they wanted was a shameful secret you could hint at but never discuss, not openly. So to people at home, Jillian was a spinster. In fact, she was as good as married to Julie, a woman who was her life partner, with whom she kept a nice house, and who loved Jillian as much as

Jillian loved her. Home home was full of people like my mother who couldn't separate a person from their sexual and domestic arrangements—which weren't really their business anyway—and whose judgment was flawed regarding anything they couldn't understand. "Different," to my mom, meant "unacceptable."

My eyes started leaking and I could feel my face getting hot and swollen as I tried to hold in my screaming, boiling rage and helplessness.

I wanted to tell my mother all these things, but I couldn't. It was one of the things I had to work on in therapy, I guess, expressing the feelings I had bottled up inside of me. But that was for another day. Today, I just wanted to scream.

Jillian's hand was cool around mine. She didn't say anything but seemed to communicate through touch: *It's okay.*

I took deep, gulping breaths as the tears rolled slowly down my hot face. "I don't want to go home," I said. "I just don't."

My mother was getting angrier by the second, especially after Jillian took my hand.

"Child, whether you like it or not, you are coming home with me when I leave. You have a week to resign yourself to the fact."

I felt like I did the time I tried to hurt her with a knife. I wanted to injure her. I didn't have a knife but I had my tongue.

"I hate you! I wish I had died when I took those pills, just so I wouldn't have to live with you ever again!" I sobbed. And, jerking my hand from Jillian's cool grasp, I ran to my room and locked the door.

A few minutes later I heard tapping on my door. From the light touch I knew it could only be Julie. My mother would have banged on the door with a clenched fist; Jillian would have tapped louder. But these taps sounded just like Julie: kind of delicate but not weak. "Muffin, open the door," she called.

I was in the midst of my enraged tantrum and couldn't move if I tried. Over the sobbing and screaming, I could hear her persistent knocking. After a while I had wound down enough to get up and open the door to her.

She didn't look happy. "Hey. You going to be okay?"

I nodded, still gulping and weeping.

"Then get out there and apologize to your mother. You've really hurt her feelings. I know you're sick but that doesn't give you the excuse to be so rude. I know you're better behaved than what I just saw."

I pushed my lips together into a pout my mother called a swell-face, turned my back to Julie, and sat down hard on my bed. "She is so evil," I sobbed. "She doesn't understand me and she doesn't want to even try. She'll never let me be happy."

"Be that as it may," Julie responded, implacable, "you still can't talk to your mother any old way. She's your mother and deserves a measure of respect."

Stubbornly, and still crying, I sat and looked at the white eyelet cotton of the comforter on my bed.

"This is not negotiable," Julie said, as softly and as firmly as she had knocked on my door.

I stood, not looking at her, and walked out to the deck. Even before I hit the back door I could hear the raised voices of my mother and Jillian, tossing angry words back and forth like the birdie in badminton.

". . . my daughter!" screamed my mother.

". . . bad mother!" rejoined Jillian.

". . . had no choice!" That was Mom.

". . . always have a choice!" That was Jillian.

Without hearing all their words, I knew somehow they were arguing about who was going to keep me. I felt weird, like a toy being fought over by children on a playground. Their voices dropped for a second and I took the opportunity to walk into the conversation.

"I'm sorry, Mom," I said without preamble.

"You should be. How dare you talk to me like that?" No easy apology where Cynthia was concerned, no sirree. I had to suffer for my arrogance.

"I don't know what I was thinking," I said, but the sarcasm flew over her head.

"No, I don't think you were thinking at all. You don't talk to me like that, ever. You understand?"

I nodded. I was starting to cry again. I turned around and went back into the house, leaving them to their argument. Whoever my next therapist was, they would have a field day with this episode, I thought.

"Look, you see how you have her so rude!" my mother accused Jillian as soon as the door was shut behind me.

"Me!" Jillian sputtered. "She never talk to me so a day in she life! I never see her get vexed once yet in the two months she here. . . ."

• • •

Back in my room, Julie was waiting for me.

"I feel like . . . like I'm on an auction block and the two of them are bidding for me with love instead of money," I said to her. "Who loves me more."

Julie carefully weighed her words before replying. "I don't think it's like that, sweetie. Your mother . . . well, she has a lot of things to offer you. This isn't about love, really. It's not in question who could love you more."

The cryptic words didn't answer any of the unspoken questions I had buzzing around inside of me. What did she mean? Was she saying my mother really didn't love me? That Jillian actually did love me more? Or was she saying that my mother loved me more but that love wasn't all that was required to take care of me?

"I don't understand, Julie. What do you mean?"

She sighed and looked troubled. "I think . . . I think your mom does love you."

It was a relief to hear it. I did have my doubts.

"But she is not good at showing her love. It comes out as criticism. I guess you could blame her family for it, if you had to blame anybody at all." She shrugged, shook her head. "I don't know. I think it was something about how they were raised. When I met Jillian she was so cold and locked away . . . it was very hard to get her to admit her feelings about anything. I think your mom is bad at showing her emotions. Believe me, Jillian knew nothing about hugging and saying 'I love you' when we first met. Thank God, she learned. Give Cynthia time."

"Time? She's had me for fourteen years and she still doesn't love me!"

Julie was firm as she corrected me. "Cynthia does love you. That much I do know. But you're sick right now, and you need a lot more attention than Cynthia gives you. I don't know if she even knows how to give anybody the kind of loving care you need. She understands duty and responsibility. Love is . . . hazy for her. She's just . . . she's just not wired that way." She had used exactly the words I did when I considered my mom and my illness. I was wired differently than my mom, and that was one of the big obstacles between us. She would never understand me or accept me.

I told Julie my fears.

She nodded slowly. Her eyes were getting a bit shiny now too. "Yes, I see what you mean. It is hard for us, too, to deal with your illness. But we are willing to try. I don't think Cynthia is. I really don't. She had you when she wasn't expecting to, and she was so young! From what Jillian tells me, your mom was never very maternal. Strangely enough, she took great care of her mother before she died. Babies are not the same as older folks, I suppose."

"So why did she have me, then?" I scowled.

"You think it's that easy to abort a baby?" Julie asked softly. "Back then it wasn't easy to get an abortion in Trinidad. It still isn't. And you know your mom is Catholic. Jillian said Cynthia never even considered terminating the pregnancy. Your grandmother would have had a cow."

She wasn't even an adult when she got pregnant. What choice would I have had, in her shoes?

I considered this. Thought about the rumors about a girl in my school who had disappeared for months and then returned the mother of a baby boy. The nasty things people said about her, even though many of them were also having sex and could have well been in her position. My mother had had me right after leaving secondary school. She had only been two years older than I was now. The thought of myself trying to take care of an infant on my own at such a young age was terrifying. I shuddered, the heaviness of the burden occurring to me for the very first time.

"I ruined her life," I despaired.

"Oh, no, honey!" Julie hugged me quickly. "Not at all. You did make it more challenging. And maybe she didn't deal with it so gracefully. She did the best she could."

The enormity of what having me must have meant to my mother's life, her opportunities, her choices weighed on me. It was something I'd definitely have to take to therapy.

"But I want you to promise me," Julie said, "no matter what happens, that you'll keep an open mind and an open heart. And if you have to go back home, you'll try to give your mom a break."

It was ironic to hear the words, but I understood what they meant. My mom couldn't really handle my illness; I'd have to do it by myself—with the help of doctors. She wouldn't be supportive. It wouldn't be the end of the world, not like if she locked me in a cage or something, but it would make my therapy much harder. One of the things I'd come to love about my temporary home in Edmonton was the unspoken support Jillian and Julie gave to me. It was there in the hugs and the occasional questions: Are you okay? Is there anything going on we need to talk about? The glances they gave me were just rich with love and affection. I didn't feel appraised when I walked into a room where they were, just appreciated.

I was dying to ask how come she and Jillian were fighting to keep me, but I didn't want to let Julie know I had overheard her private conversation. Finally my curiosity won out.

"Did you and Aunty Jillian talk about keeping me? I guess it wasn't a surprise when my mom came to take me home, since you were so prepared with your arguments."

"It was kind of a surprise," she admitted. "We knew she'd come but didn't expect her until August. I guess she felt we were letting things get out of hand when you had that last breakdown."

Her frank use of the word was jarring. I still felt sensitive about the recent excursion into my mental wasteland. My Classic Nervous Breakdown. No shame in it, just a need to prevent it from happening again, or, if it did, to make sure it was dealt with in the right way.

"Jillian really wants to have children, but I don't think we need to try to do that now," Julie said. "We're trying to start a new business, we're breaking even but not really making much money yet. . . . It's not a good time for that."

I tilted my head and looked at her. "How is it okay for me to stay but not okay for you to have a baby?"

Julie grinned. "I don't have to change your diapers, do I?"

I had to laugh in return.

"Can you imagine Jillian doing it? Since I'm the one who'll really be doing the fun stuff like that, I guess I have some say in when we have a baby."

I could see her point.

She was fingering the end of her long ponytail when a loud knock came at the door.

It was my mother. Her eyes were red. She looked at Julie and said, "Do you mind if you and I have a word outside?"

Julie nodded and left with Mom.

I waited nervously but didn't have long to wait.

When Julie came in, her wide smile told me all I needed to know.

I was staying.

I pulled up my phone and messaged Akilah and Josh: *IM STAYIN YIPEEEEEEEEEEE.*

CHAPTER
NINE

Dr. Khan gave me an exercise to do the day after my mom arrived, his last appointment before I met my new therapist. He said I should make a list of all the things I loved about Trinidad and all the things I hated about it, and all the things I loved about Edmonton and all the things I hated about it. It would help me to process this new stage in my life, he said, because even though I thought I only hated home, nothing is ever that simple.

I started with Trinidad. The things I loved: my mom, Akilah, the sunshine, the beach, the hills. It was a short list. The things I hated: my mom; school; how closed-minded people were, how judgmental, how racist, how mean. Things I loved about Edmonton: Jillian and Julie, my bedroom, the library, summer flowers, Josh. What I hated about Edmonton: everything was so strange, so big and so intimidating, and sometimes I was the only person in the room who looked like me.

When I showed Dr. Khan my list, he looked thoughtful. "You're going to work on this, okay? This is just the tip of the iceberg. Spend some time thinking about what you really miss about home, and what you really like about here. Trust me, it will help you over the next few months. Living here, going to school, it's going to be an adjustment."

Having to give up her only child—even one she had mixed feelings about—wasn't something my mom agreed to lightly. There were terms and conditions. I had to go to school. I had to go home for Christmas. And most of all, I had to swear I was returning to Trinidad at the end of a year. I would have agreed to anything short of the amputation of my limbs to hear that I could stay. I anxiously agreed to all her rules.

The arrangement did nothing for her temperament. Cynthia was sour and distant for the next five days, which was as long as her visit lasted. Even on the four-hour drive to Banff, a national park with the biggest rivers, lakes, and mountains I'd ever seen, she sat unimpressed and silent. After a joyless hour of hiking from the pretty little town up the side of a mountain, Julie and Jillian gave up on trying to delight Cynthia. The drive back was as silent as the drive there.

On the night before she left, Jillian threw her a dinner party to send her back home. Josh and his dad came.

"Mom," I said, nervously, "this is Josh. He's Jillian's godson."

She shook his hand and gave him a long up-and-down look, trying to peer past his skinny jeans and fitted T-shirt to see his soul. I could have told her it wouldn't work, and that she shouldn't judge this book by its cover.

"She's letting you stay?" he said under his breath when we went to the kitchen.

"Yeah," I replied. "Only for a year, though." I snuck a look at him out of the corner of my eye. "What about you?"

"I'm staying!" He was glowing like a lightbulb. "My mom isn't exactly thrilled, but she's willing to give me up for a year too. So you'll have company." He laughed shortly but not unkindly. As we walked back out to the deck he whispered, "Dysfunctions R Us . . ."

Julie had gone all out for this dinner. I was glad. In a way, it was not only my mom's farewell party; it was my welcome home party, too. In the dining room, I looked at the faces reflected in the yellow candlelight. Nathan—drinking a glass of water, I was happy to note—looked interested in something my mother was saying. Jillian seemed glad, too, smiling broadly and proudly. Julie, as usual, was placid and kind. And Josh looked excited and thrilled. My mother wasn't happy, I could see. She was frowning, her lips tight and turned down. But as the night wore on I could see her relax somewhat, perhaps getting used to the idea that for the next year she'd be free of the responsibility of having a teenage daughter to mind.

I wondered how I looked to them. I could guess: a little anxious, a little excited, plenty hopeful. I had a year to find my feet in this world, a year to get used to my condition and to learn to deal with being clinically depressed and having an anxiety disorder. A year to start to get better. I was ready.

I rose and slipped away into the tiny closet behind the front door where the coats were kept. I put my hand into the pocket of my Princess Di coat and took out the schedules for the Fourteen bus and the Eighteen bus, the schedules that had been my constant companions since I had come to Edmonton. I crumpled them into balls and took them to the kitchen, where I dumped them into the garbage. Julie was in there to get a fresh bottle of wine. "What's that?" she asked.

"Nothing important," I said. And it was true. I knew my buses. I could find my way home. Home home was right here.

From the other room, Jillian called, "Kayla! Time to eat!"

"Coming!" I answered. Julie took my hand and we walked outside together.

RESOURCES

Where to turn for help . . .

If you or someone you know suffers from depression or mental illness:

National Alliance on Mental Illness (NAMI)
nami.org
1-800-950-6264

Mental Health America
mentalhealthamerica.net
1-800-969-6642

Teen Lifeline
teenlifeline.org
1-800-248-TEEN (8336)

Teen Mental Health
teenmentalhealth.org

Substance Abuse and Mental Health Services Administration (SAMHSA)'s National Helpline
1-800-662-HELP (4357)
samhsa.gov/find-help/national-helpline

If you or someone you know is suicidal or in crisis:

National Suicide Prevention Lifeline
suicidepreventionlifeline.org
1-800-273-8255

Crisis Text Line
crisistextline.org
Text 741741

IMAlive
imalive.org

ACKNOWLEDGMENTS

I am grateful to God for this opportunity to write about some of his more misunderstood children, and to L.D. for graciously allowing me to use aspects of her personal story here.

Thanks to the team at the CODE Burt Award for Caribbean Writing, which caused this book to be published. Thanks to Polly Patullo and Papillote Press for your patience and kindness. Thanks to Delacorte Press for giving *Home Home* the opportunity to reach more people in its second edition, and to my excellent Delacorte editor, Monica Jean.

Thanks to the team of the Bocas Lit Fest, who have done so much for the development and support of Caribbean writers and publishing. Special thanks to Nick Laughlin: your work changes lives.

Thanks to my family and particularly my daughters, Ishara and Najja; my nephew, Taye; and my husband, Brian, for their endless love and care for me when I cannot care for myself.

ABOUT THE AUTHOR

Lisa Allen-Agostini is a widely published novelist, journalist, and poet from Trinidad and Tobago. She writes primarily about the Caribbean, its people, and its culture. Lisa lives in Trinidad with her family; her dog, Sassy; and her fabulous cat, Fennec. *Home Home* is her second novel for young adults and a Burt Award winner.

lisaallen-agostini.com

@AllenAgostini